CHAOS of CRIME

CHAOS
of
CRIME

Dell Shannon

William Morrow and Company, Inc.
New York

Library of Congress Cataloging in Publication Data

Shannon, Dell, 1921–
Chaos of crime.

I. Title.
PS3562.I515C466   1985   813'.54   84–22624
ISBN 0-688-02297-9

Printed in the United States of America

First Edition

1 2 3 4 5 6 7 8 9 10

BOOK DESIGN BY PATRICE FODERO

This one is for
Jacintha Buddicom
because she likes Mendoza best

What a chimera, then, is man! What a novelty, what a monster, what a chaos, what a subject of contradiction, what a prodigy! A judge of all things, feeble worm of the earth, depository of the truth, cloaca of uncertainty and error, the glory and the shame of the universe.

—PASCAL, *Thoughts*

C h a p t e r 1

There was a man turned into wolf prowling the streets of downtown Los Angeles these nights.

He didn't know he had turned into wolf. He thought of himself as an eminently sane and rational man—only different from other men.

But there was always a cold, small place in his mind that was aware—aware that if anyone should find out, other men would take him and do terrible things to him—lock him in a cell, and perhaps even kill him—so he was always very careful. He had always been very careful—except that once. That had been the first one here, and it had been stupid and impulsive. He had ruined a good suit—he wouldn't do one like that again.

There would be times when the days went along and he was content, and then the Voice would begin whispering to him again, and he would know it was time for another one. He didn't clearly remember how long it had been since the last one—but all last night the Voice had been talking to him, so he knew it was time for another. Today when he had come to work he had brought his tools, locked away in the little case in the trunk of the car.

He was a meticulous, accurate workman. All day he had sat at the desk at his work, with the anticipation of the next one at the back of his mind, and now it was five minutes of five and the end of the working day.

9

He folded away the papers he had been working on in the manila envelope, and put them into the desk basket tidily. He put the cover on the calculator.

The man at the desk next to his stood up and stretched. "I wonder what the temperature went to outside," he said. "It's early for a heat wave to get started. And now, for God's sake, we buck the rush-hour traffic on the freeway. Thank God it's Friday— I'll be glad to get home tonight."

"Yes," said the man turned into wolf in his pleasant low voice. "It can be bad. I think I'll stay downtown for dinner and avoid the jam."

"You carefree bachelors—you can please yourselves."

They rode down in the elevator together, with other people. In the lobby the other man said, "Well, good night—see you on Monday."

The man turned into wolf went out the plate glass door of the tall building into the hot glare of the blazing cavernlike street, the big buildings on all sides. Other people were streaming past, heading for the parking lot. He stood on the sidewalk, undecided, and then started up for the next block on Flower Street. There was a nice restaurant there where he often had lunch and sometimes dinner.

With daylight saving, the sun was still fairly high. He had some time to kill. It wouldn't be dark until nine o'clock or so, and he couldn't go hunting until after dark.

"Jesus H. Christ!" said Pat Calhoun, and drew in his breath with a long hiss. "I saw the photos of the others, but the real thing—"

"Not pretty," said Hackett.

And this was number five. Number five since the last day of April, and this was the second week of June.

You could just see that the thing on the bed had been human, and a woman. The head had been cut off and was sitting on the second pillow on the double bed; both eyes had been gouged out and deposited beside the head. The entire genital area had been sliced away and left between the outspread legs. The lower torso had

10

been disembowelled, the intestines torn out and draped across the footboard of the bed. Both the breasts had been sliced off and left beside the corpse. And there was the trademark—the carved cross between the breasts, as on all the others.

This was number five—all of the others bearing that same trademark, and of course there was nowhere to go on it.

"We'd better get out of here and not mess up the scene for the lab," said Hackett.

"Not that they've given us anywhere to go," said Calhoun. They went out to the hall of this shabby, cheap apartment on San Marino Street. Hackett said, "You okay?"

Calhoun said roughly, "Don't be a damned fool, Art—I've seen my share of messy accidents—and homicides, for God's sake."

They had all seen their share. It was cops got called to look at the bloody messes. But when they had landed here ten minutes ago, they had found the patrolman who had taken the call—Dave Turner, hardly a rookie and a good man—vomiting into the gutter. Hearing that it was number five, they had told him to put a call into the lab.

Now they just stood in the dusty hall of this ancient apartment house, disinclined to talk to the witness, waiting for the lab men to show.

"And there won't be any leads on it, any more than the others," said Hackett.

"Damn all," said Calhoun.

Number five—and as usual Headquarters Robbery-Homicide had this and that going on to work, but this was something else. Hackett stood there looking at Calhoun, waiting for the lab men to show, and thought about the other four, and the various things they had going on to work.

A few changes had come to Headquarters Robbery-Homicide since the first of the year. They had lost Sergeant Lake in February, shot by the amateur heister, and Administration had given them Sergeant Rory Farrell to sit on the switchboard, with one of the girls from Communications, Rita Putnam, sitting in on his Sundays off. Then in March the Narco office had lost two men—

11

one shot fatally during a wholesale drug bust and one retiring after thirty years' service, and Administration had arbitrarily plucked Henry Glasser out of Robbery-Homicide and transferred him up there. On Mendoza's bitter protestations that Robbery-Homicide was just as shorthanded as Narco, finally in April Administration had given them Calhoun as a replacement. Calhoun was one of the bright boys shooting up in rank early; he had only ridden a squad four years before making plainclothes detective at twenty-six, and he was barely thirty now. He was a big, handsome, wide-shouldered fellow with curly dark hair and a charming one-sided grin; nobody could help liking him, but Hackett and Higgins at least were still regarding him with some reservation. He had a mind like quicksilver and was rather given to erratic conclusion-jumping. But Mendoza liked him very much; of course they were essentially the same kind, relying on emotional instincts rather than cold logic. Calhoun had been at the Robbery-Homicide office at Seventy-seventh Street Division the last four years and wasn't exactly an inexperienced detective.

Scarne and Horder showed up, lugging all the lab equipment, and heard that it was number five. "Oh, Jesus," said Scarne, looking sick.

"All I can say is," said Hackett, "if you have to throw up, don't do it on any evidence."

"Not that we've turned up any evidence for you on the others," said Horder sourly. They went into the apartment.

"I suppose we'd better talk to this girl," said Hackett.

The door to the apartment across the hall was open, and they could hear the girl still crying. This was a very typical old apartment building for this area—small, shabby, one-bedroom places. The building was sweltering hot, without air conditioning. It was fairly early for a heat wave to get started, but it could happen any time in southern California. They went across to the other apartment.

The girl who had found the body was sitting crouched in a chair still sobbing and hiccuping. The tenant here was an elderly man named Braun, looking bewildered and shocked. The girl was in her mid-twenties, blond, and fairly good-looking.

"We'd like your name," said Hackett.

She sat up and looked at him forlornly. "Marlene Thomas," she said.

"And who was she?"

"Nadine Foster. We were going to lunch together—I was picking her up—I got a car and she didn't." She sobbed.

And of course they knew, but it had to be spelled out. "She was a hooker—in business for herself—maybe like you?" said Calhoun.

She sat up and dragged a hand over her face, smearing her eye make-up. She was too sick and shaken to be at all wary, and she would know they weren't Vice cops. She said dully, "That's right—but oh, my God, to see her like that— Oh, my God. Neither of us—meant to go on hustling—rest of our lives—just like me, she come out here hoping to get into show business, but it's not so easy—and you've got to live— She was savin' up, goin' to take a course at a beauty college and get a decent regular job—"

"All right," said Hackett. "Do you know where she usually picked up the johns? Do you know where she was going last night?"

"No—no, I don't know." She was a thin blond girl with a long nose and pale blue eyes. "I don't know— She had a card up at all those porno places down here, like me, but if she didn't get the date set up that way she'd hit any of the bars— She didn't have a car like I say, it'd be the places along Olympic, Alvarado, Wilshire— No, I didn't see her last night, I was supposed to pick her up at eleven this morning—and the door was unlocked, I just went in—see her like that, oh, my God—"

And Hackett thought, the lab would be getting photographs of that head, but they couldn't show those around. "Can you give us a description of her? Height, weight, age?"

She looked at them uncomprehendingly. "What do you mean? Nadine— She was twenty-six— I guess about my size— Call it five-five, a hundred and twenty."

13

The man didn't know a thing. He was an old bachelor, retired from some probably humdrum job, and he said he didn't know anybody in the building, all younger people, working people. There wasn't anybody else at home in the place. They would have to let the night-watch men ask questions, whether anybody had heard or seen anything, but it wasn't likely.

There would be no leads on it at all, as there hadn't been on the others.

Marlene Thomas said she could get home all right, she had her car. They got her address and let her go. They went out and stood on the sidewalk; Turner had gone back on tour. It was blazingly hot in the street. "Handful of nothing," said Hackett. "No way to go hunting, Pat."

"And this is a something, isn't it," said Calhoun. "Another Ripper." He lit a cigarette. "Nowhere to look. The hookers, for God's sake, it could be anybody in town. The advertising cards and the porn shops—" He hunched his wide shoulders. They knew how that went. The owners of the porn shops would charge a little fee for putting up the cards on the bulletin boards, wouldn't pay any notice to the casual customers maybe copying down the phone numbers. Aside from that, the girl wandering around the local bars looking for pickups—it wasn't very likely that any of the bartenders would have noticed which anonymous john she had picked up last night, if she had. And it was just getting on for noon; none of those bartenders would be on until around four o'clock. They would have to go through the motions and ask around, doing the legwork, later on; but it would come to nothing.

"Write a report on it," said Hackett. "The lab hasn't given us a damn thing, and won't on this."

"Where do we go looking for a lunatic?" said Calhoun savagely.

They had, of course, looked in the indicated places, when number two had showed up. They had asked the computers down in Records for any similar M.O., and drawn blank. They had asked the institution at Atascadero—for the criminal insane—about any recent ones let loose who might be suspects for mutilation mur-

14

ders, and come up with nothing. They hadn't gotten the autopsy reports and lab reports on these in a hurry; there was too much scientific work to do on them. And when they got those reports on this one, it would be more of the same.

At the moment, there wasn't anything to do on this but write the report. Later, canvass the bars, and probably some of the bartenders would have known her as a hooker, but it wasn't likely that any one of them could say, yeah, she picked up a john here last night, and give a usable description.

They drove back to Parker Center in Hackett's Monte Carlo. Farrell was sitting on the switchboard reading a paperback. In the communal detective office, Wanda Larsen and Nick Galeano were listening to witnesses, Jason Grace on the phone, everybody else out somewhere. It was Landers' day off.

"I want to kick this around some more with Luis," said Hackett.

"He's not here," said Farrell. "When he heard the new call was number five he collected all the paperwork and went to talk to a head-doctor at the Norwalk facility. Not that I suppose the head-doctor can tell us anything useful."

"Damn it, probably not," said Hackett. "You can write the report, Pat."

"Thanks for nothing," said Calhoun. "And goddamn it, after looking at that damn bloody mess I don't know that I want any lunch."

Hackett was feeling about the same way. He glanced around the office and asked Farrell, "Nothing else new down?"

"Just witnesses coming in. That Stripper—and a couple on the latest heist at the liquor store last night."

Wanda was listening to the witness on Jack the Stripper. That one had been around since the first of the year, and they had nicknamed him as a joke; now, with a for-real ripper in their midst, it seemed a rather sick joke. He had been hitting the all-night gas stations on Central beat and in Hollywood and Hollenbeck divisions, cleaning out the register and getting the attendants to strip, walking off with all their clothes. The latest couple of times he had hit in Hollywood, but last night he'd pulled a job at a station on Alvarado, and the victim had just come in to make a statement. He was a paunchy middle-aged man named Simms, and he was still mad.

"Of all the goddamned things," he said to Wanda, "stealing all my clothes! My God, it's one thing to get heisted, but leaving me stripped naked—I mean, it's crazy! Well, all I can say, he was a young fella, maybe five-ten, medium build, with sort of dirty blond hair—"

Which was, of course, the same description they had heard before. He signed a statement when Wanda had typed it up.

Palliser was talking to the witnesses on the liquor-store heist, and what they had to say was interesting but rather useless. The witnesses were Albert Preston, the owner of the store, and his clerk, Don Meehan, and they were both still surprised and outraged.

"I tell you, Sergeant," said Preston, "you never saw such a good-looker—a real beaut! She's maybe just in the teens, real young, and she's absolutely gorgeous, see?—a figure like one of these models in *Playboy,* real curvy, a real eyeful, see, and she's got this bright red hair down to her shoulders, natural I mean, you can tell— She had on a white pantsuit, kind of tight—and she's a real beauty, a real gorgeous dame. I was never so surprised in my life, see. They come in, and I had it on the tip of my tongue to ask for I.D., because they both looked so damned young and I'm not about to risk my license sellin' to minors—and then this girl, she pulls a gun out of her purse and says to clean out the register—it was a pretty big gun—and she says, all business, snap it up, buddy, I'm a crack shot and I'd just as soon get some practice in on you—"

"She sure as hell meant business, all right," said Meehan.

"And neither of you noticed much about the man," said Palliser. This was the second time they'd heard about the gorgeous redhead with the gun.

"Not much," said Preston. "I tell you, the girl was sort of takin' up all our attention, know what I mean? He was just a punk kid—another teenager, maybe, I couldn't tell you what he looked like. But he took the money when I handed it over."

"And you didn't follow them out to see whether they got into a car?"

"We did not, Sergeant. It was a pretty big gun, and that redhead was all business."

Palliser laughed, but that was another handful of nothing to work. The businesslike redhead and her anonymous partner had pulled a heist at another liquor store last weekend. The description hadn't turned up in Records, and there was no way to go looking. As usual, Robbery-Homicide had several other heisters to look for, and a couple of bodies to do the paperwork on, if nothing very mysterious—the overdoses, the derelicts passing out of natural causes. He took statements from both men; there was always the ongoing paperwork. When they'd gone out he went over to Hackett's desk to hear about the new one.

"Number five," said Hackett. "My God. And the lab won't give us anything more than they did on the others."

Calhoun was slouched at his desk smoking, with his long legs stretched out. "The bloodthirsty lunatic, and he could be anybody, anywhere. What little we can guess about him takes us nowhere."

Palliser perched a hip on a corner of Hackett's desk. "Replay of the Ripper," he said. "The hookers, and all the mutilations. Nowhere to look. Five in six weeks, my God. When we get the lab and autopsy reports, they'll say the same things. And the lunatics don't always go around foaming at the mouth."

"I suppose we go through the motions," said Hackett. "The legwork. Go and talk to those bartenders when they're on duty. But we all know those dives—they're dark as hell, and who's going to notice the anonymous john the hooker picked up? And it could have been a date made by phone, the john getting her number from the advertising card in one of the porn shops."

"That's about the size of it," said Calhoun.

17

"And I really don't suppose," said Hackett, "that Luis is getting anything useful from the head-doctor."

Higgins and Galeano came in towing a suspect for questioning, and Higgins stopped at Hackett's desk to hear about number five. Hunching his massive shoulders, he said, "God. Nowhere to look."

"Don't say it, George. The cheap hookers, I suppose no loss, but that one's a real maniac, he ought to be locked away. What have you and Nick come up with?"

"Possible on that pharmacy heist on Wednesday night." Higgins followed Galeano down toward the interrogation rooms, and the other three just sat there thinking glumly about the lunatic.

"Those bartenders won't be on until around four," said Hackett again.

"And how many bars," said Calhoun, "she might have hit? Alvarado, Glendale Boulevard, Sixth, Wilshire—my God. If it wasn't a john just calling to set up a date."

It was exactly the same setup they had faced on numbers two, three and four—the prostitutes who might have met the john anywhere, and no telling where. They had all had the advertising cards placed in the porno shops, they would have all picked up the johns casually at bars around the street aside from that. They had all been living in shabby, cheap apartments, counterparts of Nadine Foster's, on the old residential side streets around Central beat. It was all anonymous all the way; but the bloodthirsty lunatic they'd like to catch up to.

At the same time, Mendoza was sitting beside the desk of Dr. Arnold Shapiro in his office at the Norwalk Mental Facility, waiting to hear what Shapiro might have to say. He had bundled up all their records, the gruesome photographs and lab reports and autopsy reports, and handed them over to Shapiro for evaluation. He sat back in the chair smoking and thinking about their lunatic, while Shapiro looked over all the paperwork, occasionally grunting a cussword.

By the little they had heard from the Traffic men, number five was a replay of the last three. Number one had been slightly different. Number one had been Brenda Sands, and she had been a senior at Belmont High School, apparently a respectable girl. On the last night of April she had been at a rehearsal of the class play in the school auditorium. It had broken up about ten o'clock. Her steady boyfriend had called for her and walked her up to the school—she lived just a few blocks away, on Loma Drive—and ordinarily he'd have walked her home; but she'd had a fight with him over another girl during the rehearsal, and started home alone. She'd been found about midnight by a householder coming home late, in a vacant lot only a block from where she lived. She'd been savagely mutilated, decapitated, disembowelled, and there had been the trademark, a cross carved deeply between her breasts.

The next three had been carbon copies: all prostitutes, and not much to choose between them. Maria Montoya, an apartment on Rockwood Street: thirty, getting to be a lush. Claire Stroud, Coronado Street, a similar apartment, forty-two with a long record of solicitation and drug use. Doris Barnes, Fourteenth Street, she'd been black, twenty-three, no record but known to be a hooker.

Shapiro slapped all the papers together back into the manila folder and sat back in his desk chair. "All very horrifying," he said. He was a youngish man with graying brown hair and shrewd eyes. "What do you want me to tell you, Lieutenant?"

"You're supposed to know this and that about lunatics," said Mendoza.

"I sometimes wonder," said Shapiro. He added after a moment, "Sex is a very funny thing."

"Now that's what I call a profound statement," said Mendoza.

Shapiro laughed shortly. He passed a hand over his hair and said, "Generalizations. You catch the lunatic and we'll diagnose him for you. But what can we say about the mass killers—the woman killers? There's the one thread running through all those cases—the sex hang-up. But it doesn't always take the same form. God knows there are enough people walking around with a

19

tendency to sadism, who'll never see the inside of a psychiatrist's office. Who'll never carry it to the nth degree of murder. And the ones who did—the ones we know about—" He shrugged. "It's a glib axiom to say those men had got to a place where they couldn't achieve sexual satisfaction without killing—but it's not altogether true. Look at them—the Ripper, Christie, Kürten, Heirens, Boost, Holmes—Landru, Petiot, Smith, Ted Bundy, Gacy— If we're mentioning prostitutes, Cream—which of them was legally insane? Even if you judge them all as insane—which probably isn't the case by any means—they were all different cases. You can certainly say they all had the sex hang-ups one way or another—with the exceptions of Petiot and Holmes, who simply killed for money—but that kind of thing isn't so easy to diagnose, you know." He shut his eyes, leaning back in the chair. "The little we know about the original Ripper, it's very possible he was a surgeon—anatomical knowledge shown in the mutilations. Christie—he was undoubtedly insane legally, though the jury didn't buy it and he was hanged. He got to the point where he could only get sexual satisfaction with a dead body. Cream—another lunatic—was altogether different. It didn't seem to be important to him to witness the actual death, he just slipped women the poison and went away. And speaking of the Ripper and Cream, I've always wondered whether they really hated the prostitutes or simply killed them because they were the available females. Boost, of course, by all we can guess, simply disapproved of sex per se. Smith was another killer for money, but he also probably disliked women intensely. It's very probable that none of those—or even De Sade himself—had what you'd call a normal sex life, but then there's Kürten." Shapiro sat up and regarded Mendoza with a mirthless grin. "Now that one was interesting."

"The Monster of Düsseldorf," said Mendoza.

"That's the one. He killed indiscriminately, both sexes, whatever was available. Just a simple thirst for blood. Talk about sex hang-ups—he told the psychiatrist that his most satisfactory sex experience had been copulating with a sheep while he cut its throat—and yet he seems to have lived a perfectly normal married

20

life for over ten years. At least his wife said so—said he was a very gentle man, and she didn't believe him at first when he confessed the killings. Haigh, now—he confessed to drinking his victims' blood, but he was trying to build an insanity defense. Manson— just bloodthirstiness complicated by drugs. Bundy— bloodthirstiness again, together with the lunatic egotism, he mustn't be prevented from carrying out any impulse. They're all shapes and sizes,'' said Shapiro. ''And there's not much any of us could tell you about this one, Lieutenant. He may be legally insane or he may not. What you call his trademark—the cross carved on the bodies—could indicate some religious obsession, possibly connected with sex. I can give you an educated guess, and it doesn't help you at all.'' He smiled. ''In every other area of life he probably looks and acts as sane as anybody else walking around. Nobody ever remotely suspected any of those men until they were caught up with. He probably functions quite normally until the urge hits him. Probably has a job somewhere. He may be married. Looking like the ordinary citizen.''

''And I could have deduced that for myself,'' said Mendoza. He stabbed out his cigarette in the ashtray. ''Simple bloodlust. And the hookers available.'' But he wondered again about the first one. Had that one just been spotted alone, and attacked on impulse? ''Thanks so much.''

And Shapiro said again, ruefully, ''You catch him and we'll diagnose him.''

By the time Mendoza got back to Parker Center it was after four o'clock. Hackett and Calhoun had gone out to ask questions at the various bars where Nadine Foster might have picked up a john last night. There hadn't been anyone at home at that apartment house except the elderly Mr. Braun; the night watch could go and ask if anybody had heard or seen anything, but that was a very long shot.

He heard about the latest heist from Palliser, and said, ''Bonnie and Clyde. The gorgeous redhead. A little offbeat.''

''And,'' said Wanda, drifting over from her desk, ''Jack the Stripper again. I wonder if it'd be any use to try to get a composite sketch. They've all given a pretty good description.''

21

Mendoza was not immediately concerned with Jack the Stripper. Robbery-Homicide had the usual caseload to handle, the heists, one unidentified body, one teenager dead of an overdose, an attempted homicide by a jealous boyfriend, a suicide; even when they hadn't any mysteries to solve, there was the never ending paperwork. Grace and Galeano were now out hunting possible heisters from Records. Mendoza smoothed his neat moustache in habitual gesture and said, "Damn it, Art and Pat are out wasting time. Nobody will have noticed the hooker picking up the john."

"Not likely," agreed Palliser, and yawned. "Saturday—what'll you bet the night watch gets called out on a couple of more heists? And maybe a new body."

"Just a little ray of sunshine," said Mendoza.

He got home early, to the big Spanish hacienda in the hills above Burbank, and on the way up the hill noticed the Five Graces—the sheep intended to eat down the underbrush—reposing picturesquely on the green slope of permanent pasture. At least their man of all work, Ken Kearney, had taught himself to shear them; last year it had been an expensive proposition to import a shearer from a hundred miles off.

The twins, Johnny and Terry, were riding their ponies around the ring attached to the corral, and he waved at them. It wasn't quite as hot as it had been on the streets downtown, and it was early for a heat wave to start, but in southern California you took the climate as it came. He went in the back door and found red-haired Alison and their surrogate grandmother, Mairí MacTaggart, chatting over dinner preparations. "Oh, you're early," said Alison. Baby Luisa, not so much a baby now at eighteen months, and as red-haired as Alison, was getting under everyone's feet in the kitchen. "Interesting day, *cariño*?"

"Interesting hell," said Mendoza. "We've now had number five. Another hooker."

"Oh, for heaven's sake," said Alison.

Mairí said, "Och, that lunatic—a terrible thing that is. And you having no clue at all to know who he is?"

"Not so far," said Mendoza morosely. *"Mañana será otro día."*

"Well, you've got plenty of time to have a drink before dinner," said Alison. The very unexpected baby, which was due at the end of October, was just beginning to show on her usually excellent figure.

"And I think I need one," said Mendoza.

Hackett and Calhoun wasted the best part of three hours wandering around those bars. Naturally the bartenders—who had known Nadine Foster as a hooker—hadn't noticed her picking up any john. The only thing they got was that she had been seen in one of those bars on Alvarado Street, last night about nine o'clock. So probably she hadn't had a date set up with one of the johns calling from the advertising card in any of the porn shops.

Hackett got home late, having called Angel to warn her of that. She'd kept dinner warm for him; the children, Mark and Sheila, were already in bed. "Well, so we've got number five," said Hackett. "This damn lunatic."

"Oh, Lord," said Angel. "The things that do happen. And I had to marry a cop."

On Saturday night the whole night watch was on—Bob Schenke, Rich Conway, Matt Piggott. The Piggotts, of course, had just produced an infant in February, a girl named Ann Catherine, and Piggott was rather fatuous about it—the bachelors, Schenke and Conway, were bored hearing about it. The advent of the infant had prompted Piggott to acquire his first camera, and he had some more rather blurred snapshots to show. "We're still looking for a house," he said, "but the interest rates—"

The day watch had left them some work to do, questioning the tenants in that apartment house on San Marino Street, and Piggott and Schenke went out to do that. Conway stayed in to mind the store and didn't get a call until seven-thirty. It turned out to be a homicide—when he looked at it, a mugging on Sixth Street with a man dead. He'd been the ticket agent at the Greyhound bus station

23

there, just leaving the job at seven o'clock. He'd been found by a fellow employee who said he'd come out not five minutes later. And it would have been just accident that he ended up dead, knocked down against the sidewalk. There were always the muggers roaming around even in broad daylight. And if anyone passing on the street had seen anything they would have averted their eyes and hurried on. There'd be no evidence on this, nowhere to go—the paperwork and that was all.

Chapter 2

Mendoza was supposed to be off on Sunday but he usually came in for a while. As expectable, Piggott and Schenke had got nothing from the other tenants at the apartment where Nadine Foster had lived; nobody had heard or seen anything, they were all ordinary working people and none of them had known she was a hooker. She'd only moved there a couple of months ago. Mendoza kicked it around unprofitably with Hackett and Calhoun, the set of gruesome photographs spread out on his desk.

"The doctors can't tell us much, but that we can deduce," said Hackett, looking a little sick. "Nothing to hear because they were bound and gagged while the torture was going on, all that prior to death because the blood was still flowing. Of course the mutilations would have caused death at some point. But the first one—"

"Mmh, yes, it looks as if it was just her bad luck she was on the street alone, and the lunatic happened to spot her—on his way to picking up a hooker? Or after gratifying the bloodlust did it occur to him that the hookers were easier prey?"

Calhoun said ruminatively, "Loma Drive. He could have been heading up to a bar on Beverly or Third, and just spotted the Sands girl by chance. He may have intended to pick up the hooker and took her instead."

"*Claro está*," said Mendoza. "All up in the air."

Hackett said, "One thing does occur to me, Luis. Is this his first

25

time out? Those were savage kills, and the urge might have hit him the first time last April thirtieth, or it might not. We've got no record of the M.O., but I wonder if anybody else has."

"I'm ahead of you, Art," said Mendoza. "It occurred to me too. Five in six weeks, *por Dios*. We'd better put it out to N.C.I.C. and ask, and we should have done it before." He went down to Communications to set that up. The N.C.I.C. hot line carried particulars of all current crimes and criminals to every law-enforcement body in the country. If anybody had any knowledge of the lunatic's M.O., that should trigger some memories, even if he wasn't on the current wanted list.

There wasn't much else to do at the moment. Higgins and Landers were out looking for possible suspects on one heist, Galeano and Grace on another. Palliser had taken those witnesses to the liquor-store heist, Preston and Meehan, down to R. and I. to look at mug shots, but that would be an empty gesture. By the description, the gorgeous young redhead and her anonymous partner were probably too young to be in records.

The new homicide, the Greyhound ticket agent, was nothing to work either, the anonymous mugging. It could have been a couple of gang members or just the punk kids looking for an easy few bucks. If there had been any witnesses, and it would have still been broad daylight, they'd have shied off getting involved in the little scuffle, passed by on the other side. The night watch had gone to break the news to his wife up in Hollywood, and she had said he wouldn't have had more than ten bucks on him.

"It'd be a waste of time to talk to that bartender again," said Calhoun. "He just barely noticed the Foster girl there on Friday night. Couldn't say if she'd picked up anybody or drifted out alone."

Before Mendoza came back, Rita Putnam passed on a bulletin from N.C.I.C., sent up from Communications. It was about one Oliver Buckley, with a long and bad record of armed robbery and assorted violence. He had escaped from a work detail at the federal pen in Indiana yesterday; he'd been doing a five-to-ten for bank robbery. It was possible that he might be heading west, his home town was L.A., and he had a half-brother here, one William Martin, address appended, Grandview Avenue. Martin had corresponded with him and might be inclined to offer him aid and comfort. Buckley was described as Negro, six-one, a hundred and ninety, black and brown.

"Well, he can't be here yet," said Calhoun, "but I suppose we ought to talk to Martin and ask cooperation."

Hackett lit a new cigarette and said, "There's time."

The other employee at the Greyhound station, who'd found the mugging victim last night, came in to make the formal statement, and Calhoun typed it up. Higgins and Landers brought in a possible suspect and wasted half an hour talking to him; as it often happened, it was all for nothing, no solid evidence, and the victim admitted he wouldn't recognize the heister. They let him go and sat down at their respective desks. Landers was yawning his head off.

"You have any bites on the house?" asked Hackett idly.

"Need you ask?" said Landers. "Nary a bite. That damned place—Phil being the penny pincher." With real-estate prices being what they were anywhere closer in, Phil—whose parents hadn't known she'd turn into a policewoman when they christened her Phillipa Rosemary—had seized on the house in Azusa as a bargain, and of course it was just too far away. It took Landers an hour and a half coming and going on the freeway, and the month after they'd moved they had put it up for resale, but they were still stuck there. "I suppose we should praise heaven for small mercies. Phil coming back to work this week, at least we're both on day shift and can ride together." Phil's car had finally given up the ghost last month. She'd been on maternity leave for the last six months, since the arrival of Sara Ellen last December, and of course speaking of small mercies they had discovered Mrs. Jacobsen right across the street, who had raised seven of her own and was very willing to babysit Sara Ellen all day.

There were more possible heist suspects to look for, but none of them felt inclined to leave the air conditioning for the glaring hot streets. They sat on for a while talking desultorily before Higgins said reluctantly, "Well, this isn't earning our pay, I suppose we

27

ought to do some work," and got up. Hackett went out with him.

Mendoza was reading the bulletin from N.C.I.C. "So we ought to contact this Martin sometime, and it's likelier we'd find him home on Sunday."

"There'll be time to do that," said Calhoun lazily.

And then Rita came in and said, "You've got a new homicide."

"Oh, hell," said Calhoun. "Where and what?"

"It's at a laundromat on Alvarado," said Rita. "The Traffic man's holding some witnesses for you."

It was the usual bare, sterile-looking laundromat, and the squad-car man was Don Dubois, very tall and black and efficient. He said to Calhoun and Landers, "This is the damndest thing I ever saw. People. You sometimes wonder if we've made any progress since we stopped living in caves."

There were four witnesses, all female, huddled around one of the tables, and the body of a man on the floor in front of one of the dryers. They looked at him, and there wasn't a mark on him. He was an ordinary-looking man wearing brown pants and a yellow T-shirt, and he hadn't been dead long, he was still warm. Dubois said, "This is Mrs. Diggs, she's the one called in."

She was a big fat woman with dyed red hair, and she said, "It's just a terrible thing, all of us here saw it, it's just terrible but none of us knew either of them, we talked about it while we waited for the police. We never saw either of them before. I know Mrs. Robinson here, we usually do our laundry about the same time on Sundays, but I don't know these other ladies and they say they'd never seen either of them—the other one, he was a young fellow too, and we hadn't paid any attention to them before it happened, we were all just doing our laundry, you know—I'd just taken a load out of one dryer and put another one in—"

"So what happened?" asked Calhoun.

The second woman was thin and dark. "Well, they got into a terrible argument about the dryer. You can see that one dryer's out of order, it usually is, it's a nuisance if there are many people here. And that one"—she nodded at the body—"he'd just taken his

28

laundry out of the washer and brought it over to the next dryer, it was the only one wasn't being used, and the other man came up with his wash at the same time and they started to argue over who got to use it first—''

"For God's sake," said Landers. "Were they together, do you think they knew each other?"

The fat woman said, "Oh, I don't think so, they hadn't come in together. And that one on the floor, he hit the other one, they were both cussing and swearing, and the other one knocked him down and he fell against a dryer and I guess he hit his head an awful crack."

"And then that one," said the other woman, "he just grabbed up all his wet laundry and ran out—''

"For God's sake," said Landers again. They took a look at the corpse, and both of them having seen a number of corpses they could guess that the man had fractured his skull on the hard surface of the dryer. There was I.D. on him; he'd been Joseph Tronowsky, of an address on Burlington Avenue. By the driver's license he was twenty-seven. The women couldn't offer anything but a vague description of the other man. There wasn't much point in getting the lab out on this. Dubois called the morgue wagon, and they told the two women they'd want statements, no point either in getting those from all four of them. They were cooperative. "You got to help the cops," said Mrs. Diggs. "As soon as we get our laundry out of the dryers—''

Calhoun told them where to come. The morgue wagon carted the body away and then he and Landers went to look for the address on Burlington to break the bad news. It was the usual ancient apartment building and it seemed there wasn't anybody to break the news to. They only turned up one tenant who had known Tronowsky, another young fellow named Rubioso, who had the apartment across the hall. He could tell them where Tronowsky had worked, at a garage on Hoover, but he didn't know about any relatives, he'd only known Tronowsky casually. Calhoun had taken the billfold and keys from the body; they let themselves into the apartment and looked around. It was an anonymous shabby place, and there wasn't an address book or any letters anywhere around. Just some clothes in the closet, and in the chest of drawers in the bedroom a bankbook from the Bank of America showing a total of four hundred and three dollars in a savings account. The billfold held his Social Security card and driver's license and a little over twenty bucks.

"Dead end," said Calhoun.

"We can ask at the garage," said Landers. "Somebody might know about relatives."

The garage, of course, was closed on Sunday, but they got the emergency number off the door and talked to the owner on the phone. His name was Weaver and he was conventionally sorry to hear Tronowsky was dead but more annoyed than anything else.

"He was a goddamned good mechanic, and you don't find one like that on any street corner. Well, he'd worked for me about six months. He come out here from some place back east, Illinois or somewhere. I never heard him mention any relatives."

"So, not much to do on this one," said Landers. "Not a hope of dropping on the other one—just a silly damned accident, the fight over who got to use the dryer."

They went back to the office. Mendoza had already left, and the two women had just come in to make the statements. The paperwork had to be done and filed away for the records. At least, Tronowsky had had enough money to pay for a funeral.

Palliser got home early to the house in Hollywood, and was greeted by the big black shepherd, Trina, on the service porch. Roberta was sitting at the kitchen table over a fat cookbook, and as he bent to kiss her said, "Slow day, I take it."

"Enough on hand but nowhere much to go on anything," said Palliser, shrugging off his suit jacket. "It must be a hundred on the street. Thank God for air conditioning." Davy came running up, discovering he was home. "It's a thankless job, Robin."

"And don't you dare wake up the baby, John. I've just got him to sleep, he's been a pest all afternoon."

But Palliser went down the hall to look at the baby fondly, anyway. They'd both rather hoped for a girl, but you took what came, and the baby, Alan John, was a nice addition to the family.

Higgins was glad to get home to the big house in Eagle Rock. It was murder on the street, close to a hundred, and he just thanked God for air conditioning in the car. At least, the traffic on the freeway wasn't so bad on Sunday. He came in the back door. Mary was taking dishes out of the dishwasher, and he kissed her soundly. Laura Dwyer was pounding the piano in the living room, and their own Margaret Emily came trotting to be picked up.

"Steve's out in the darkroom," said Mary. "You'd better go and warn him dinner's nearly ready. Interesting day, George?"

"Are they ever?" asked Higgins tiredly. "Just more of the same. I'll go call Steve." One of these years, after he'd finished high school and college, Steve Dwyer would be joining the criminal lab team downtown. "And this damned lunatic running around, no handle on it at all."

Mendoza had said, something catching going around the office, the wives producing babies all at once. Galeano, kissing Marta in the kitchen and going down the hall, grinned to himself; the joke had been on Mendoza, discovering unexpectedly that they were due for a new one too. Galeano, who'd come to the domesticities a little late, regarded the offspring fatuously: a very pretty one she was, Christine Maria, just turned two and a half months old, pink and plump and serenely asleep in the crib. He shed his jacket and tie and went back to the kitchen.

Marta was pouring wine over shaved ice. "You didn't wake her? I will have to keep an eye on you—you will spoil her to death, Nick. Sit down and relax. You had the rough day?" She'd never lose her little German accent.

"Just the usual," said Galeano.

At about eight o'clock Patrolman Bob Gunther was cruising down Figueroa on his regular tour. He was still technically a

31

rookie, on the job just ten months. He was proud of being an L.A.P.D. man, of wearing the uniform and doing the job. He'd never had any other ambition than to be a cop, and he was a conscientious cop and meant to make rank on this force. He had just had his twenty-third birthday last week, and he was engaged to be married to a pretty girl named Linda.

He was cruising along slowly, his ear turned to the radio for any calls coming his way, keeping an eye on the street. But on Sunday night there wasn't much traffic down here, wouldn't be until later when the theaters let out and the restaurants began to empty. He had just passed the intersection of Pico when the car ahead of him turned up the next side street, turning the wrong way into a one-way street—he could see the sign from where he was, and that driver was either drunk or blind not to spot it. Gunther stepped on the gas and turned after him, switching on the siren briefly. The car was an old Buick, and obediently it pulled over to the curb.

Gunther got out of the squad, putting on his cap. He just glanced at the license plate to check that it was out-of-state. He didn't intend to write a ticket unless the driver was under the influence. He went up to the driver's door and the driver rolled down the window. "May I see your license, sir? You just made an illegal turn, this is a one-way street."

The driver was a young fellow, dark and good-looking. He didn't look or smell to be drunk. He didn't say anything, but brought out a billfold and slowly took out the license from its plastic slot and handed it over. Gunther started to say, "I'm not going to write you a ticket, but just watch it—" and he felt only immense surprise when suddenly there was a gun in the driver's hand. He heard it go off, felt the hard slam of the slug hitting his chest, and fell over backward onto the blacktop. He didn't hear the Buick take off.

That was a narrow old residential street, but close enough to the Stack where all the freeways came together, and to busier main drags, that it wasn't the quietest place in town. It wasn't until ten minutes later that a home-going resident of the apartment building on the corner happened on the body and the squad-car beyond it.

32

The girl sitting on the switchboard in Communications was startled at the rough male voice in her earphones. "Say, is anybody reading me? I don't know how to work this damn thing— Is anybody there?"

She said crisply into the mike, "Give me your call number, please."

"How the hell do I know what it is, but somebody ought to hear, there's one of your cops dead in the street here, looks like he's been shot. It's Mitchell just off Figueroa, I was just comin' home and spotted it—"

On Sunday night the night watch was all on; weekends were apt to produce business for Robbery-Homicide. Schenke and Conway shot over there, and found the honest citizen waiting for them. His name was Smith. He said, "I don't know a damned thing about it, I was just on the way home, and here's the police car and the officer lying in the street. I wasn't sure how to work the radio, but I got through all right. No, there wasn't a sign of another car anywhere around."

They thanked him, got his full name and address, let him go. It was still broad daylight. And there in the hot glare of the westering sun the uniformed man looked incredibly young, staring at the sky with open expressionless eyes. It looked as if he'd been shot in the heart, in the body anyway, and maybe died instantly. The I.D. told them his name. There wouldn't be any work for the lab to do until the coroner's office got the slug out of him.

But Schenke bent closer over the body and said, "My God, look at this, Rich." There was something clutched in Gunther's right hand; Schenke pulled it loose and stood up. It was a driver's license. It had been issued to Jerome Carpenter at an address in Santa Barbara, and it had expired six months ago. By the description, Carpenter was Caucasian, twenty-four, six feet, a hundred and seventy, brown and blue.

"For God's sake," said Conway, "he'd just pulled him over for some reason and the bastard shot him? Of all the damned stupid senseless things—"

33

The dispatcher sent out a car with an extra man in it to ferry the squad in. Schenke and Conway waited for the morgue wagon and then went back to headquarters and asked some questions in Communications. By what they got there, Gunther hadn't had a call on anything since coming on swing watch at four o'clock. He'd only called in a Code Seven, out to eat, at seven o'clock, and reported back as available at seven-thirty.

Schenke raised somebody at the coroner's office and told them to go for the slug as soon as possible, send it over to the police lab.

On Monday morning, with Palliser off, that was waiting. Mendoza said softly, *"Por la gracia de Dios!* But places to go on it—"

"Just where?" said Calhoun. "There isn't a car registered to him." That, of course, had been the first thing the night watch had asked about; Sacramento hadn't any record of a car for Jerome Carpenter.

The Traffic watch commander, a Lieutenant Reed, had been waiting for them when they got in, and he was a very angry man. "That was one damned good man, Mendoza, one of the best we'd got this last year. He'd made the highest grades of his class at the Academy, and he had the hell of a good record since he'd been on the job. Just running into this goddamned bastard by chance—"

"From what the night watch tells us, it looks as if he pulled a car over, maybe to write a ticket or just warn the driver. Jerome Carpenter." The driver's license was on Mendoza's desk. "And very damned obliging of him to leave us his name, wasn't it?"

"By God," said Reed. "You'd better drop on this one or I'll go hunt him personally!"

Hackett laughed mirthlessly. "And if we do, you know what he'd likely get. Maybe he's hair-trigger, maybe he was drunk, maybe he just doesn't like cops—in any case, it wasn't premeditated."

Mendoza stabbed out his cigarette. "Don't we all know," he said coldly. "Voluntary manslaughter, and he'd spend about nine months in and get out on P.A. But there's no use swearing about

34

it—fact of life—there it is. We'll pick him up if we can find him, *compadres*.'' When Reed had gone out, still swearing, he got on the phone to the lab. "Has the coroner's office sent over that slug out of the Traffic man yet?''

"It just got here," said Scarne. I suppose you want a make on it right away. Without putting it under the 'scope I'd make it a heavy caliber, probably a thirty-eight. I'll get back to you when I've had a closer look."

"Santa Barbara," said Higgins. "He could be back there by now."

"Or on the run in some other direction," said Landers savagely.

"And I don't think," said Mendoza with a snap of his lighter, "we get that phone number and ask politely if he's home." He got Farrell to put him through to Santa Barbara headquarters and talked to a Lieutenant Contreras who did some cussing to hear about their patrolman. "You might send a couple of men to that address to sniff around," said Mendoza, "and have a look in your records for him."

"All too happy to oblige," said Contreras. "I'll do that, and get back to you as quick as possible."

There were still the heisters to look for; Higgins, Landers, and Galeano went out reluctantly on that. It must be up to a hundred degrees again on the street. Five minutes later Dr. Gable of the coroner's office called Mendoza. "My good Christ," he said. "This new body—or what's left of it—you'd better catch up to this werewolf, Lieutenant."

"We'd like to," said Mendoza irritably. "Tell us how. What can you tell us about it?"

"Not much more than we could tell you about the other four," said Gable. "About the most gruesome human remains I've ever had the misfortune to examine. My God, what a mess. Well, this one died anywhere between nine and midnight Friday night. It's probably going to be impossible to say whether there'd been sexual intercourse before or after death. Impossible to say exactly what killed her, the decapitation or the mutilations. Most of the mutilation was done while she was still alive. Christ."

35

"Vaya por Dios," said Mendoza. "But you thought that on the others too. Which must say that they'd all been gagged in some way, or they'd have screamed their heads off—apologies, I didn't mean the sick joke—and the latest four were in small apartments, they'd have been heard."

"My God, what a thing," said Gable. "We're still running tests as best we can for any semen in or on the body, and I suppose your lab's looking at the scene."

"And they'll probably come up with nothing," said Mendoza. "What we can deduce from the latest three, and this'll probably be a carbon copy, the lunatic isn't so lunatic, except when he's killing. The evidence is that after they were dead and his bloodlust satisfied, he washed up very thoroughly before he left—the residue of blood, same type as the victims, in the basin in the bathroom, bloodstained towels. I think it's probable that he strips naked to do the torturing and killing, so there wouldn't be any blood on his clothes. But the first one, of course, looked a little different."

"My good God," said Gable. "You haven't got any line on him at all? Well, if we come up with anything else we'll pass it on."

Mendoza put the phone down and said, "So here we are again, Arturo. No useful evidence. A werewolf, the man says, and that's a name for this one."

There had, of course, been stories in the press, but played down, and they hadn't released some of the evidence to the press. The trademark of the carved cross, for one. On the bloody killings like these, they occasionally got the fake confessions, and it was useful to know something the fake confessors didn't. But the word would be out on the street, among all the hookers, and they'd all be running scared.

"Another thing," said Hackett. "The pattern—the pattern on those four, they were all in business for themselves, not tied to any pimps."

"Claro está," said Mendoza. "He's not a lunatic all the way, Art. Just as the head-doctor said. He's being very careful not to be noticed. He looks for the ones like that, he isn't going to get him-

self noticed by the pimps setting up the dates. I'm inclined to think the Sands girl was an impulsive kill. He just happened to spot her there on the street, and pounced."

"That's what it looks like," agreed Hackett.

Landers and Higgins came back empty-handed. Calhoun was perched on a corner of Wanda's desk talking to her while she tried to get a report written.

They were all about to take off for lunch when Contreras called Mendoza back.

"It looks like it's no dice here, Lieutenant. I went out on it with one of my sergeants, and Carpenter hasn't lived at that address for eighteen months. It's his mother's house, and she's a good type, has a decent job, she's the upright citizen and cooperated. She's worried as hell about him. He's A.W.O.L. from the Army since about six months ago. She said she'd hoped the Army would straighten him up—he's never been in police trouble, but evidently he's the kind never holds a job long, cadges money from her. So far as she knows, he doesn't have a car, the heap he was driving before he joined the service had to be junked. You said there's nothing registered to him."

"Gunther didn't take down the plate number. It could have been borrowed or stolen. Did you ask if Carpenter's got any pals down here?"

"Not so far as she knows. She hasn't seen him in eight months. An Army officer came asking after he'd gone over the hill, but she couldn't tell him anything. She gave us the names of a couple of fellows he'd run with last year, but they're both in regular jobs here and claim they hadn't heard from him since he'd been in service. Sorry it's a dead end."

"Thanks anyway."

"I hope to God you catch up to him," said Contreras.

"Just hold the good thoughts on it, *amigo*."

Just after they got back from lunch Scarne called to tell them about the slug. It was a .38, and out of a Colt revolver. Which was interesting to know but of no immediate use. Higgins and Landers went out resignedly on the legwork again, and Calhoun, slouched in the chair beside Mendoza's desk, said lazily, "I suppose somebody ought to look up that William Martin. The relative of the escaped con. We've got the address somewhere, haven't we?"

"It's on our beat somewhere. If the con's heading our way he probably isn't here yet. Unless of course he pulled a new job somewhere and collected enough loot for an airline ticket." Mendoza wasn't much interested.

And then Farrell came in and said, "There's a bank job just gone down. Security Pacific on Wilshire."

"No rest for the wicked." Mendoza stood up and reached for the perennial black Homburg. In the big office he passed that on and added, "Come on, Pat, we'll leave Nick to mind the store in case business picks up some more."

"Don't I count?" asked Wanda sweetly.

Calhoun grinned at her. "The beautiful blond detective. You're just for decoration, darlin'."

Wanda put out her tongue at him and said, "You go to hell." Calhoun just laughed and followed Mendoza out. Time had been when the feds had handled the bank jobs exclusively, but these days they left them largely to the local boys while sitting in.

Galeano leaned back in his chair; he was studying Carpenter's driver's license. The photo on it was only about an inch square but fairly clear. It was a boyishly handsome face with a weak chin and wide-set eyes. "You know," he said thoughtfully, "I wonder if the lab could do anything with this—blow it up for reproduction in the press. If this bastard's still around somewhere, somebody might recognize it." He stood up. "I think I'll take it up and ask."

Wanda was just sitting there at loose ends ten minutes later when Farrell relayed a call to a new body, so she went out on it alone. When she got there and looked at it it didn't look like anything abstruse to work; they seldom did get the mysteries. Depending upon what the autopsy report said, probably just more paperwork.

It was in the parking lot of a high-rise professional building nearly out of Central's area, and it was the body of a rather elderly-

38

looking black man dressed in neat sports clothes. The patrolman was Frawley, and he said, "There's a witness, but it doesn't look like much of anything."

The witness was an excitable young woman with a frizzy blond frosted wig and a fretful baby. Her name was Adele Elrod, and she said, "Are you a policewoman? I thought all of you just did office work for the regular cops." Wanda suppressed rage; you had to be polite to the citizens. "Well, what happened, my goodness, the poor man, we'd had an appointment with Dr. Shepherd, I mean Randy had, this is Randy—you be good now and stop crying—he's our pediatrician—and when we came out just now, I'd had the parking ticket validated in the office, and I drove around to the exit and the man came to take it and just as he took it he got the funniest look on his face and all of a sudden he keeled right over and fell down, and I don't know if he had a heart attack or what—Randy, stop yelling, honey—but I figured I ought to tell somebody so I parked again and went in and told the receptionist in the ground floor office and she called the cops—"

There was I.D. on him for Edward Jackson, an address on Bronson Avenue in Hollywood. By the driver's license he was sixty-eight; it could have been a heart attack or stroke. In any case, it wasn't anything for the lab. Wanda told Frawley to call the morgue wagon. By then the building superintendent had come out, hearing about it, looking concerned. "My God, Jackson—he'd been our lot attendant for twenty years, a very steady man—this is a damned shame—dropping dead all of a sudden—well, of course it's an easy way to go— Yes, he was married, had quite a big family I think, he was quite a family man—"

One of the jobs they came in for was breaking the bad news. Wanda saw the body off in the morgue wagon and started up to find the address in Hollywood. That little job would take her to the end of shift.

Late on Monday afternoon, Hackett found himself with an hour to spare before the end of shift. They had about come to the end of the list of possible heist suspects on the current cases. Of course neither of the victims had come up with a make on the gorgeous redhead and her anonymous partner; that figured, they'd be too young to show in Records or have mug shots on file.

Mendoza and Calhoun were still apparently out on the bank job, and nobody else was in. Hackett sat ruminating about their Ripper, and the hell of a thing it was to ruminate about, and presently remembered that N.C.I.C. bulletin. The escaped con, Oliver Buckley, and the half-brother he might contact here if he headed west.

He found the bulletin and took down the address. It was in the Westlake area, not far away. Of course on a weekday Martin might still be at work, if he had a job.

It was an old six-unit apartment building, and William Martin was at home, in a rear second-floor apartment. He looked at the badge in surprise and asked, "What do the police want? Oh, come in. You said Sergeant, well, sit down and say what I can do for you." There was a tiny tan Chihuahua yipping impudently at Hackett. Martin was a tall thin fellow, medium black, probably in his thirties, neatly dressed in casual sports clothes.

Hackett told him what it was about, and he looked alarmed. "Oh, my Lord," he said. "Ollie getting away like that—my good Lord." He sat down in one of the two upholstered chairs and the little dog jumped into his lap. "I just don't know what to say, Sergeant."

"Do you think he might be heading this way—that he might try to contact you?"

Martin was stroking the dog automatically. He said in obvious distress, "I guess I got to say, maybe. You wonder what gets into people, Sergeant. Maybe the power of Satan. Ollie—it just makes you wonder. All of our family's always been good decent people, hardworking and respectable. I got a good job, I'm one of the cooks in the kitchen at St. Vincent's Medical Center, today's my day off. I'm not married, I guess you could say I live a kind of quiet life, there's just me and Pancho here." He rubbed the Chihuahua's ears affectionately. He had a mild face and gentle eyes. "Ollie—I don't know why he went wrong. He's ten years younger than me.

My own dad was killed in an accident when I was only five, and then Mother married Mr. Buckley, and he was a good man, a lay preacher in our church—Grace Baptist—but he got cancer and died when Ollie was only about ten.''

"You'd been in touch with him—your half-brother. Since he was in prison."

Martin nodded. "Yes, sir, that's right. I promised Mother on her deathbed that I'd always do whatever I could for Ollie. Whatever he did, however bad he was. I don't know why he went wrong, did all those criminal things, bank robberies and I don't know what all. I've got to say, Sergeant, I'm some scared of him—he can be a right dangerous fella—but I promised Mother I'd do whatever I could for him, you see. Since he'd been in prison this last time, I'd wrote him, I sent him little things he asked for—cigarettes and such—and I always sent him some tracts from the church, you never know when maybe the Christian message will reach a man. But—'' His Adam's apple jumped nervously and the hand stroking the little dog was suddenly shaking—"I'm right sorry to hear Ollie's loose. I—I got to say it could be he'd come to ask me for help. He knows I'd help him, for Mother's sake. But I'm an honest man, Sergeant, I wouldn't go against the law.''

"Well, if he should contact you, if you should find out where he is or anything about him, we'd like to know.'' Hackett tore a sheet from his notebook, scrawled his name and the office phone number on it. "We'd be obliged if you'd call in, if you hear from him.''

"Surely, Sergeant, I'd do that. I'm an honest man, and Ollie, he's been a grief to the whole family. I don't rightly know why he went wrong.''

Chapter 3

On the night watch nothing went down for Piggott and Schenke; Conway was off. They sat listening to the police frequency, and Piggott looked idly at real-estate ads in the *Times*. He and Prudence would like to find a house at a reasonable price, which was probably a vain hope. There was business for Traffic on the street, and they did some talking about that patrolman that had been shot last night, but nothing came their way the entire shift.

On Tuesday morning, with Calhoun off, Mendoza and Hackett came in early to find one of the feds waiting for them. All the feds were the same, whatever they looked like, urbane and neatly dressed in conventional business suits. This one was Gerber, one of those turned out on the bank job yesterday. He had the photographs with him, snapped automatically by the bank's cameras, triggered by a fast-thinking teller. There had been two men on that job by what they'd heard yesterday, and the bank would still be reckoning up the figures, but the consensus was that they'd got away with somewhere around ten thousand bucks. Gerber sat down in the chair beside Mendoza's desk and passed on the photos. "We've been comparing mug shots," he said, "and these aren't exactly passport photos, but this pair could be Price and Unger. Roger Price, Arnold Unger. They're on record with us from three other bank heists, all in California. They're just out of the pen about four months ago, they did the full time."

Mendoza and Hackett looked at the photos, which certainly could have been clearer, and Mendoza said, "Well, you should know your own customers."

"You can take it from there, find out about cars and so on. They're both local, hail from L.A. originally, but there aren't any relatives around." He had copies of the original mug shots to show; they studied those and agreed that the rather blurred action shots taken by the bank could well be Unger and Price. They were both white men in the thirties, tall and dark. Gerber hung around until Hackett went down to Communications to ask Sacramento about any car. Sacramento didn't show a car registered to either of them. "So that's that," said Gerber, looking annoyed. "They could be anywhere around, or long gone by now. You can put them on N.C.I.C. for what it's worth."

The heat wave had subsided a little today, and for once there wasn't much on hand to work; they'd run out of possibles for recent heists. Hackett added Price and Unger to the N.C.I.C. hot list.

Jason Grace came in late with some new snapshots to show. Their little Celia had just had a birthday, and she was a cute one, the solemn brown little girl with pigtails and red ribbons. A couple of autopsy reports came in, nothing to work, that overdose last week and another derelict dead of natural causes on Skid Row. Wanda was typing up the report on the latest one, Edward Jackson; that had probably been a natural death too and no follow-up necessary.

The morning dragged on, and at about eleven o'clock, Marx came in with a glossy print still damp. "I don't know if this'll be any use to you," he said. "Galeano had the idea of trying to blow up that driver's license photo for reproduction. I took a couple of shots at getting a decent negative, but it could be the hell of a lot clearer."

They looked at the resultant print and Mendoza said, "It's not that bad, I think anybody'd recognize him."

"The best blowup I could get was a five by seven," said Marx.

43

"Get the press to run it," said Hackett, "it could give us a break. I'll take it over to the *Times*."

They all went up to Federico's on North Broadway for lunch, and when they got back everything was still quiet, nothing down. Mendoza said, "Either feast or famine."

Then at two o'clock Farrell relayed a call, two new bodies. Hackett and Landers went out to see what it was.

The address was Sunset Place, and it was a small old single house with a patch of dead lawn in front. The Traffic man was Zimmerman, and he was on the front porch waiting for them. He was looking grim. He said, "It was the mailman called in. I let him go back on his route, but I've got his name for you. He said these people didn't get hardly any mail, just Social Security checks, and there'd been some trouble about those a few months ago. They'd had a couple of them stolen out of the mailbox, and we got called on it— I remembered that when he told me, I got chased out here to ask about it, but there wasn't anything to do on it. It was probably juveniles from the neighborhood, and I never heard whether the checks got cashed or if the people got them reissued, with all the government red tape probably not. The hell of a thing, this is. The mailman said he delivered a letter here about six days ago, first mail they'd had in over a month, and today he had a letter for them from the Social Security office—probably something to do with the stolen checks—and the electric bill. He says the Social Security checks for this month and last month had been taken in from the box, but if you want my guess they'd been stolen too. And this letter he delivered about six days ago was still in the box, so he rang the doorbell and didn't get any answer, and thought there might be something wrong. They were both pretty old and might be sick. So he called in." Zimmerman grimaced. "The hell of a thing. I thought I better take a look, and they're both dead." He led Hackett and Landers around the little house. It had been shut up, windows and doors closed, and the hot stale air inside met them in a wave. "God knows how long they've been dead, but a while."

The tiny kitchen was neat and clean; down a short hall they came into a small square living room. There was some ancient shabby

44

furniture, and the body of an old man sagging in a wheelchair. "My God," said Hackett. There wasn't any smell of death, he'd been dead too long for that, the body shrunken and starting to mummify. He was wearing a bathrobe and cloth slippers.

"The other one's in the front bedroom," said Zimmerman.

That one was an old woman, lying on the bed, and it looked as if she'd been dead about the same length of time. She was a little thin old woman with sparse white hair, in a blue nightgown.

They looked around, and on top of the cheap chest of drawers in front of the bedroom window was a sheet of paper torn from a lined tablet with a few lines of scrawled writing on it. There wasn't any salutation. *This is the only thing I can see to do, I can't go on taking care of him no longer and I am so tired, it's best for both of us we die now, we lived too long.* "My God," said Landers. On the bedside table was a dirty glass and beside it a plastic bottle with a prescription label.

"Demerol," said Hackett. There wasn't much to say about this.

The mailman had left the letter in the box; it was addressed to Mr. and Mrs. John Dunlap, and bore a return address for a Mrs. James Hutton in Greencastle, Indiana. And of course it was nothing to call out the lab on. Zimmerman put out a call for the morgue wagon and after it had taken away the bodies they went back to the office.

Hackett asked Information and got the phone number for that address, talked to Mrs. Hutton in Indiana. She cried briefly, hearing about it, and said, "Oh, I should have written Aunt Grace oftener, but you know how it is, I got four grandkids to look after, my daughter's divorced and works a regular job, and my husband's been kind of poorly. I never could find the time. I know Aunt Grace had been worried about how to go on, Uncle John was an awful burden to her, he was eighty-four and she was eighty-three, and he was part paralyzed from the stroke he had a couple of years ago, and she had the arthritis awful bad. I'd told her she ought to find out about getting into a nursing home where they'd both be looked after, they hadn't much money but the state would have paid for it, but she said they wouldn't take charity, they'd always looked after themselves. I'm just awful sorry to hear about this, they should have been in a good nursing home, but that was a terrible thing for her to do, and it wouldn't exactly have been charity, would it, that was a wrong way to think."

Hackett asked, "Will you be arranging for a funeral, or would you like us to see to that? There'll be mandatory autopsies, you understand. They don't seem to have had a bank account." There had been forty dollars in the old woman's handbag.

"No, I guess they'd just cashed the Social Security checks and lived on that. I don't know what to say, I'm afraid we couldn't afford to pay for a funeral. Of course I'm grateful you called to tell me, it's just a terrible thing, but we couldn't afford—"

"The city will take care of it, Mrs. Hutton."

Landers was looking angry. "What gets me," he said, "what about neighbors? It looked as if they'd lived there the hell of a long time, Art. There must have been people around who knew them, knew the old man was helpless, how old they were, that she had to look after him. They didn't have a car, how did she get out to shop for supplies? The nearest place is a little market a couple of blocks away, it must have been damned hard for her to get up there on foot—you'd think that somebody around there would have noticed that she hadn't been seen in a while. My God, it looked as if they could have been dead for a month or more."

"People," said Hackett. "People in a big city, Tom. They don't notice, or if they do they don't do anything about it. Don't want to get involved, invite trouble. I'll tell you what gets me—the doctor." The name on the prescription label was Dr. Hilbrand. Hackett got out the phone book. "No car and not much money, they wouldn't have gone far afield for a doctor." There was a Dr. Adam Hilbrand listed at a medical clinic on Beverly Boulevard, and he dialed. He had an argument with a snippy-sounding nurse, kept demanding patiently to talk to the doctor on police business, and finally got him. Hackett told him about the Dunlaps, and Hilbrand had to think hard to recall the name. "How long was it since you'd seen either of them, doctor?"

46

Hilbrand sounded young and impatient. "I couldn't tell you exactly, there wasn't any need for them to see me regularly, both just chronic cases— Age and general disability. The Demerol, well, I prescribed that for the old lady's arthritic pain, about all I could do for her."

"You must have realized how difficult it was for her to take care of the old man alone."

"Oh, I suppose so," said Hilbrand indifferently. "I'd suggested a while ago that she should find a nursing home, but evidently she hadn't looked into it. I'm very sorry to hear about this, of course. Will I have to appear at an inquest? Damn it, I'm a busy man."

Hackett said equably, "We'll let you know, doctor." Putting the phone down, he said, "Christ Almighty, people! The time used to be when doctors had some personal concern for their patients. I hope some of them still do, but you wonder." And this would make more paperwork and they'd have to clear things up as best they could in the absence of local relatives. Apparently the Dunlaps had owned the little house; had there been a will? There hadn't been an address book in evidence. Hackett swore and said, "Getting absentminded in my old age, I should have asked the woman." He called Mrs. Hutton back.

She said, "Yes, that's right, they owned the house, about all they had, and Aunt Grace had told me they'd left it to me, they never had any children. I don't suppose it's worth much."

Hackett wouldn't take any bets. An old street in a poor section of town, but any real estate anywhere in Los Angeles these days— she might be in for a surprise. "Do you know what lawyer drew up the will?"

"Oh, dear," she said, "I'd have to think. Aunt Grace mentioned it but— It was a Jewish name, I think a name out of the Bible—Lazarus, that's it."

Hackett looked in the phone book again and found Lazarus and Cohen at an address on Sixth Street. He called, but the girl who answered the phone said they'd both left the office. Hackett suddenly realized that it was after five o'clock. "Tomorrow," he

47

said. "And nothing moving, we might as well knock off early."
Mendoza had already left.

Landers might knock off early, but he had to wait for Phil. He
went down to R. and I., where she was just back to work, and
while he waited he thought glumly about the house in Azusa. They
wouldn't get rid of the place, and out from under the monthly payments, for God knew how long. At least they should be able to find
an apartment for less than the monthly payments, but now they'd
started a family they'd both like to have a house.

Phil came out at five of six, his cute little blond Phil with her
freckled nose, and said, "You're not looking very cheerful, Tom.
For heaven's sake don't worry about the house, we're bound to sell
it eventually, and then we can look around for a used car in decent
shape."

"At least," said Landers, "we're both on day shift. I was just
thinking—of course you never know how children are going to
turn out, but with any luck Sara Ellen will see we don't end up
alone and friendless. And if we produce another one, all the better
chance."

"And what prompts that morbid little idea?" asked Phil.

So on the long way home to Azusa, in the rush hour traffic, he
told her about the Dunlaps.

Surprisingly, in the middle of the week the night watch got some
business, but as the heat started to build up, so did the crime rate.
They got a call at nine o'clock to a heist at a liquor store on
Temple, and when Schenke and Conway got there they found an
ambulance parked in front. The patrolman was Gibson. He said,
"They took a shot at one of the owners, I don't think he's too
bad." The paramedics were just strapping a man onto a gurney,
and another man was hovering anxiously.

"You'll be okay, Dave, you're not hurt bad—but my God, what
a thing—" The paramedics took the other one out and Gibson
said, "These are the detectives, Mr. Vasquez—Detective
Schenke, Detective Conway."

48

He was a thin dark man about forty, and he transferred attention to them distractedly. His English was unaccented. "The hell of a thing," he said. "My God, these kids starting to turn into criminals as soon as they're out of the cradle these days. A girl—my God—"

"So what happened?" asked Conway.

Vasquez leaned on the counter behind him and brought out a handkerchief to mop his forehead. "My brother and I, we own this place together, he's David, I'm Anthony. We don't have a night clerk, usually spell each other. It was about half an hour ago, this pair of kids came in, they couldn't be over seventeen, a girl and a boy, my God, and Dave looks at me, I know what's in his mind, they're minors and we couldn't sell them anything but the candy or gum—they came up to the counter, and my God, the girl brings a gun out of her bag, the hell of a big gun it was, and she says, this is a stickup, boys, let's have everything out of the register. And neither of us believed it, she's a real beautiful girl with lots of red hair, couldn't be over seventeen—and Dave, well, I know how he felt, he said, now, baby, you don't mean that, and he reached for the gun—she was just a kid—and she shot him. Bang, just like that, she got him through the shoulder—and she says to me, I'm a crack shot, buddy, and I mean business, you hand over. So I did. By God, I did. My God, just a young girl—"

"Bonnie and Clyde again," said Conway. "Could you describe the boy?"

Vasquez shook his head. "Not too good, I guess. He was taller than her, I guess he had dark hair. He didn't say a word, she did all the talking. I'd have to check the register tab to be sure but I think they got away with about three hundred bucks."

"Do you think you could describe the girl well enough for one of our artists to get a sketch?" asked Schenke.

He looked slightly dubious. "I don't know, I'd sure be willing to try." The other victims had given a graphic description; everyone who'd seen her had been impressed by the gorgeous redhead, and it was worth trying. They'd leave that to the day men. "Say, where did they take Dave? I better go see how he is—"

And of course, for what it was worth, they would now get a make on the redhead's gun, with the slug out of Vasquez. They followed him out to the Emergency wing at the California Hospital, and Schenke talked to an intern, explained about the slug. "He's not too bad," said the intern, "lost a little blood is all. We'll dig out the bullet for you."

He came back in fifteen minutes and handed over the slug in a glassine envelope. Schenke looked at it and said to Conway, "It looks as if it could be a forty-four or forty-five. What the hell's a girl doing with a cannon like that?"

Bill Moss, cruising on night watch, hadn't had a call since he came on tour. He was rolling slowly down Flower Street at two-thirty A.M., the downtown streets empty and deserted at that hour, and he was thinking grimly about Bob Gunther. He hoped to hell the front-office boys would drop on whatever bastard had killed Bob. He hadn't known him well, but it had been the squad Gunther had ridden on swing watch that Moss took over at the end of that shift, and they'd exchanged some casual talk. Gunther had been a good man. And to get it like that, just the chance encounter with the hair-trigger citizen—well, they all knew it could happen.

The radio came to life and it was a call for him, a 459. He heard the address and uttered a few choice cusswords aloud. Burglary be damned, that place again, and he knew what it was—Belmont High School, the alarm sounding off back at the station. But it was like the boy who cried wolf, you had to treat it as if it were for real because it just might be. And so as usual he'd better call a backup, just in case it was. He put in the call, turning up Sixth Street. Belmont High School, and of course that reminded him of that girl. That poor damned girl— He'd been the one to take that call— the girl, all cut up and decapitated in that empty lot a couple of blocks from the school.

He slid the squad into the curb in front of the school and a couple of minutes later another squad pulled up behind him and Sanchez got out of it. They both stood on the sidewalk with their flashlights out and Sanchez said, "You know what the hell this is."

50

"We both know what the hell it is," said Moss, "but we can't just ignore it."

"For God's sake," said Sanchez, "it's the fourth time in the last month, you think somebody responsible for the damned school could do something about it."

"And the one time we just let it go," said Moss, "it'd be the real burglars."

There had been some burglaries at the public schools, the burglars after the expensive office equipment. They checked the front entrance, which was intact, and went around the main building checking all the doors, which were locked, looking for broken windows. "Where the hell's that security guard?" wondered Sanchez. With the vandals around, the Board of Education had hired security guards at night. They found this one sound asleep in the back of his car in the rear parking lot, and woke him up.

He blinked at the uniforms, getting out of the car. "Has that damned alarm gone off again? Everything's okay, it's been quiet as a grave, no trouble."

"And how would you know if there was, dead to the world here?" asked Moss. "Come on, come on, let us in."

Grumbling, the guard went up to the rear door of the building with them, and unlocked the door. The building was silent and empty-feeling. Moss and Sanchez went directly down the corridor to the box on the wall which housed the expensive burglar alarm system. "So let's see if it took more than one this time," said Sanchez. The guard fumbled for the right key and unlocked the front of the box, and as it swung open something very small fell out of it and landed on the floor at their feet without a sound. They turned the flashlights on it.

"Just one," said Moss disgustedly. One tiny mouse, electrocuted and limp.

"For God's sake," said Sanchez. "Can't the principal or somebody do something about it? The fourth time in a month. The goddamned mice chewing the wires and setting off the alarm! And the taxpayers picking up the tab whenever the electrician has to come out to fix it."

51

"Well, I suppose they've put down poison or something," said the guard. "But with all the stuff in the cafeteria, and the trashbins all around, I guess the damned mice just keep coming. You know mice. And they come out at night. You wouldn't think they could get into the box, but they can get in anywhere. They're what you call nocturnal, they come out at night."

"I know, I know," said Moss irritably. Every time the mice had set off the alarm it had been in the middle of the night.

They went back out to the street and he radioed in the result of the call, and he and Sanchez went back on tour.

On Wednesday morning the early edition of the *Times* ran that blown-up shot of Jerome Carpenter, but on the third page. It had been an idea, but it was doubtful if it would turn him up. There was no telling how long he'd been here, who the car had belonged to, whether he knew anybody here at all. If the car had been stolen, there'd be a want on it and it should be spotted eventually, hopefully with Carpenter in it.

The autopsy report on Gunther came in just after they'd all got into the office, and of course it was short and simple. He'd been shot through the heart.

"Which doesn't say that Carpenter's a marksman," said Mendoza, brushing his moustache in annoyance. "He wasn't two feet away from Gunther. And Bonnie and Clyde have showed up again, there's a witness due in to make a statement. Another heist went down an hour later." He passed the night report on to Higgins. It was Hackett's day off.

In fact, two witnesses came in on the redhead, both the Vasquez brothers. Dave Vasquez said he hadn't been hurt much, it was more the surprise than anything else. That beautiful young girl, and the gun. The slug had lodged in his upper arm.

Calhoun typed up a statement for them to sign and Higgins said, "You told the other detectives you'd be willing to try a session with the police artist, try to get a good sketch of the girl."

"Sure," said Anthony Vasquez. "I guess we could both give you a good description of her, Sergeant. She's a real looker, one beautiful chick. But my God, running around pulling holdups and shooting people—you cops ought to catch up to that one." When they'd read and signed the statement Higgins took them downstairs and settled them with one of the artists and the Identikit.

Before that a lab report had come up on the gun, from the slug out of Dave Vasquez. It was a .44 caliber and had been fired from a Smith & Wesson revolver. "*¡Dios!*" said Mendoza. "That's a big gun for a little girl." The second heist had been at a twenty-four-hour convenience market, and the night clerk wouldn't be coming in until this afternoon.

Just to clear that away, Landers went over to the office of Lazarus and Cohen the first thing that morning. Joseph Lazarus was as dapperly tailored and polished as Mendoza, a small neat dark man with an unexpectedly deep voice. He listened to what Landers had to say, and had to rummage in the office safe. "I'd forgotten the name," he said. "John and Grace Dunlap. That's one hell of a sad tale, isn't it? Poor little people. I remember them halfway." He had found the will, left in his keeping. "They just came in off the street. It's a very simple will—they hadn't any relatives except this niece. About all they had to leave was the property."

"The niece doesn't seem inclined to pay for a funeral," said Landers.

And Lazarus said simply, "Cheapskate. The least she could do. I expect she'll want to sell the house when it's through probate. I can arrange that for her, of course."

"It's not much of a house, but I suppose it'd be worth something."

"With rents what they are? And close in downtown—maybe seventy-five grand," said Lazarus.

Landers said, "The least she could do is pay for a funeral."

"Leave it to me," said Lazarus sadly. "We can deduct it from what the house brings. Let me know when the bodies can be released. I'll be in touch with the niece."

* * *

53

Just after Mendoza had got back from lunch Marx came in with the completed lab report on Nadine Foster's apartment. "There's not much in this for you," he told Mendoza. "God, what a butcher-shop that was to go over. This one's a real madman, isn't he? It looked just about like the other three. You said you think he may strip naked to do the butchering, and cleans himself up right there afterward—that's what we can deduce from the evidence. It's all spelled out here—a little blood on the bathroom floor, bloodstained towels. All the blood is her type, O. There weren't any sperm stains on the bedding or anywhere else. Which may or may not say anything—it could be he gets his kicks just out of the torture and mutilation. God. And we didn't pick up any identifiable latents anywhere in the place but a few of the girl's."

"*¡Cómo!*" said Mendoza. "And even if he'd left any, I don't think he's in anybody's records, this one." The lab had picked up some latent prints in the other girls' apartments but none of them had been on file anywhere; they probably belonged to the casual pickups, the johns, but in case any of them belonged to their werewolf, the lab would have them filed away—in case they ever caught up with him.

"And something else occurs to me," said Marx seriously. "I mean, you're the detectives, we're just the scientific boys paid to look through microscopes. But—April thirtieth, May eighth, May sixteenth, May twenty-seventh, and now June ninth. Is he getting the urge oftener?"

Mendoza was swiveled around in his desk chair staring out the window. "Oh, that had occurred to me too, *amigo*. It had indeed," he said softly. "*Dios mio,* and not a single lead to him! He's sane enough to be very careful about that."

When Marx had gone out, Mendoza read over the lab report in detail, folded it tidily on the desk blotter, and sat staring into space. He thought about what the head-doctor had said. The werewolf, looking as sane and harmless as any ordinary man walking down any street, quite possibly working at some ordinary job, mingling with people every day, and nothing about him to cause any suspicion that he was different from his fellow creatures. And

54

yet, whatever the legal state of that mind, sane enough to be careful, sane enough to know that he mustn't arouse any suspicion, leave anything behind to reveal his identity—or he'd be stopped from gratifying the bloodlust. Mendoza swiveled around in his chair again, surveying the Hollywood hills in the distance, sharply outlined and dustily brown in this hot season, and swore to himself.

Presently he went down the hall to the communal detective office to see what was going on. Nothing much was. For once there wasn't much on hand to work, but from long experience they all knew that business would be picking up after the lull.

Nobody had called in to say they'd recognized Carpenter's photo in the *Times*. There were the A.P.B.'s out on the bank heisters, Price and Unger, but without a plate number attached that wouldn't be much use. And the capsule history of their werewolf had been out on the N.C.I.C. hot line since Sunday, but nothing had come in from that either. It still could come.

He said that to Landers and Calhoun, passing on the lab report. "I've just got the growing feeling that the werewolf didn't suddenly conceive the bloodlust out of the blue. He could have killed other women in other places."

Calhoun didn't bother to look at the report, handed it on to Landers. "And I've got the same gut feeling. He's been off the rails for a long time. Only not looking that way. This is just more of what we got on the others, you said."

"*Condenación,* and just nowhere to go." Mendoza had just sat down at Hackett's desk and lighted a cigarette when Farrell relayed a call. A heist, at a market on Olympic. "*Por Dios,*" said Mendoza, "I can remember when the heisters used to wait until after sundown." For want of anything else to do they all went out on it, and it was a handful of nothing. There had been two heisters, both black, both with guns. Four of the check-out clerks had been off on their lunch break, and the four witnesses—all female—had been too scared to notice much of anything about the heisters. They said vaguely that they were both pretty big and meanlooking, had on just ordinary clothes, they hadn't noticed any scars or particulars. And there were, in L.A.P.D.'s records, quite a number of big black men with pedigrees of armed robbery who might have pulled this job, but it would be looking for the needle in the haystack, take a month of Sundays to haul all those in and lean on them in the hope that one of them would come apart and admit it.

When they got back to the office from that unprofitable exercise, an autopsy report had come in. It was the report on that senseless accidental homicide last Sunday at the Laundromat: Joe Tronowsky. He had, of course, died of a fractured skull. "Just another stupid damned thing," said Landers. "The argument over who got to use the dryer first. And I suppose it's possible the other one never realized Tronowsky was dead. Got in a snit and ran out with his wet laundry. Sometimes I wish I'd taken my father's advice and gone in for veterinary surgery like him."

The witness to the other heist last night came in about three o'clock, and Galeano talked to him. His name was Carlos Gonzales.

He said nervously, "I can tell you what he looked like, mister. *Dios,* you wouldn't forget one like that in no hurry, see." Gonzales wasn't very big: He had a narrow dark face and a prominent Adam's apple. "The manager, he tells us don't put up no fight to the stickup guy, just hand over, the place is insured. But, *Dios,* I wouldn't have tried to put up no fight to that one , no way, anyways. He was a big black guy, must have been about six-three, and he had a big gun. And *Santa Maria,* he's real weird-looking, you know? He's got this great big bushy Afro and he's got a gold earring in one ear, and he's wearing another gold ring in his nose, God's sake—real weird—and I kind of think he was high on something, way he talked. Believe me, mister, I just handed over what was in the register, I wasn't about to argue with him."

Galeano stopped taking notes and said, "Now you don't tell me. But—well, there couldn't be two like that, that's got to be Benny Troutman, but I thought he was in jail." He beckoned Jason Grace over. "Jase, you put the arm on that Troutman guy

56

about ten days ago—I sat in on the questioning—it was armed robbery, an independent drug store somewhere.''

"That's right," said Grace. "It was his third count on that, he's got a little J.D. record too, possession, assault, a string of petty stuff. Why?''

"Well, he ought to be still in jail waiting for the hearing, but apparently he isn't, he pulled another heist last night.''

"Do tell," said Grace. "I wonder how in hell he made bail. Nobody in the family's working, and with his mother's taste for cheap gin the welfare money doesn't go so far.''

"We'd better find out. At least we'll have an address for him.'' Galeano called the jail; Troutman had made bail last Friday.

"Well, God knows he's not very smart," said Grace amusedly, "but you'd think he'd have had sense enough not to do another job before he's put up before a judge. Or if he wanted to, to get rid of the earring and nose ring first. These stupid punks.''

The address for Troutman was Thirty-eighth Street. Grace and Galeano drove down there, and found him at home. He was watching TV with the rest of the family, his mother and three younger sisters, and they were all half drunk. He was annoyed and surprised at the cops dropping on him.

"How did you make bail?" asked Grace interestedly.

Troutman said in a growl, "Oh, God's sake, my steady girl friend, she sold her old car, get me out. Now it's just wasted. Goddamned cops.''

"Only yourself to blame," said Grace, grinning. "You really haven't got much sense, Benny.'' They ferried him back to the jail. He had some reefers on him, only about four dollars in cash. Gonzales had said he'd taken about a hundred bucks on the heist; maybe he'd given it to the steady girl friend in gratitude for the bail. They would wait until tomorrow to apply for the new warrant.

When Higgins had left that morning he'd told Mary not to expect him for dinner, he'd stay downtown and get in a little shooting practice, which he hadn't done in a while. Tomorrow was his day off but he'd just as soon not drive downtown then. He'd pick up dinner somewhere and get in an hour's practice on the range. They were all expected to keep up a certain standard of marksmanship. He'd brought along some extra ammo.

He picked up a *Herald* and went to a restaurant on Wilshire. Glancing over the paper, he found a brief story about a couple of British cops ambushed and shot by a couple of hoods in London, and he thought those British police were either the bravest bastards or the goddamndest fools on the face of the earth, walking around on duty without sidearms. The very idea scared him. It wasn't once in a blue moon you had to draw the gun, but if the occasion arose, the gun was there; even off duty, you were required to pack the gun.

He got up to the range at the Police Academy at seven-thirty. There were quite a few other men there, and he had to wait for an alley to be free. All the L.A.P.D. men used this range and a lot of other departments roundabout. While he waited, he got talking with a couple of Traffic boys from Hollywood Division, Rutland and Martinez. They treated him a little deferentially, the important detective sergeant, which annoyed him some; they were all cops together.

After a while Rutland was saying, "Sometimes you get the funny things happening, one thing about this job, you never know what to expect. I had a thing this afternoon—I was cruising down Kingsley and this woman hails me. She's the prim prissy type, she says this woman down the block's been making up to her little girl and gave her a present, and she doesn't want any part of it, it's probably stolen anyway, and the woman wouldn't take it back just now and when she saw the squad she thought she'd better hand it over to us. Crazy—just nothing."

"Females," said Martinez.

"What was it?" asked Higgins idly.

"Oh, a gold necklace with an old-fashioned locket sort of thing. There was a name engraved on it—Martha Deere. She insisted on handing it over, and what the hell could I do? I turned it in to the watch commander at the end of shift."

It was just a vaguely queer little story, but for some reason it rang a faint bell in Higgins' mind. In a fuzzy sort of way, it seemed to be connected to a name—a funny sort of name.

One of the alleys got free and the Hollywood men let him take it. The Department wasn't fussy about what you carried as long as it was regulation heavy caliber; he packed the S. & W. Combat Magnum .357.

A rather unusual name—an old-fashioned locket—

He got off five measured shots, the classic stance, right foot forward, using the combat grip. They all placed respectably near the center of the target. And then, just as he squeezed the trigger to empty the gun, the wires connected in his mind and he said aloud, explosively, "Naudsinger!" The shot went wild and hit the top of the target.

Chapter 4

The man turned into wolf was on his way home from the job. He'd stayed downtown for dinner, avoiding the rush-hour traffic. Just for the time being he was content, but he felt vaguely that the Voice might begin to whisper to him very soon again. Right now he was thinking back to the latest one, savoring the remembered pleasure, and beyond to all the others. He remembered them all in such clear detail. His mind roved back a long way, and he thought again about the first time he had experienced the ecstasy, the ecstasy of the blood. He had been eighteen then and on the way home from school, when he had seen the little girl in the street, all smashed and mangled by the big truck, and he had been vaguely aware of the other people around, screaming and excited, but the beautiful warm sensual waves possessing his body had occupied all his attention. The ecstasy had come to him then, he had dreamed about it for months afterward, and began to imagine ways to create the ecstasy for himself. But of course he had never been able to do anything about that until his mother had died and he was alone in the house.

He had found the books in the library, the books about the other men who had understood the ecstasy, but he couldn't bring them home because she'd have found them, and it wasn't as good just reading at the library because he wasn't alone there, and he had to be alone to experience the greatest surge of the ecstasy—alone, or with the thing that he used to achieve that. Sometimes he'd got away, by saying he was going to church, to see one of the films, the ones with all the blood. After she had died and he had the house to himself things had changed; it was then he had begun to do the things to bring the ecstasy. He could bring the books home then and go to see the films, some of them he had gone to see over and over.

And he had found out about the animal shelters. He'd never heard about them before, but the woman next door had brought home a little dog and said that was where she'd gotten it, and the idea had been so exciting, so absorbing— He had gone there the next day and bought the dog, the first dog. It had made quite a lot of noise, but the basement was solid and well insulated, and nobody could have heard it. After that he'd found there were a number of animal shelters in the city, and he'd bought the dogs and some cats, until he'd gone back to one place too soon and the attendant had asked him some sharp questions about the puppy he'd got there a couple of weeks before, and he'd said it had got run over, and the man had been reluctant to sell him another. He had even enjoyed the cleaning up afterward, all the blood, and going out at night to bury what was left of the bodies in the backyard. But he'd stopped going to the shelters then. The small, cold place in his mind was aware that nobody must ever suspect that he was different from other men, that he was one of those singled out to know the ultimate ecstasy of the blood, other men not understanding would punish him for that.

But it was not long after that that the Voice had come to him, compelling and insistent, telling him what it was he must do to achieve the most powerful ecstasy.

He remembered in clear and loving detail the first one, and all the others, in that place and other places. He dwelt on them, savoring the remembered sensual surges of pure joy.

By then he was back in his apartment, and he had all the books to read; he had bought all those he could and stolen others from the libraries. But tonight he felt that the books could not altogether satisfy him. He sat thinking back to all those he had used to bring the exquisite ecstasy, and after a while, just as he had expected, the Voice began to whisper to him in his mind, far away as yet, but it would get louder and more insistent. *The great whore that sitteth upon many waters, the mother of harlots and the abominations of the earth—the flattery of the tongue of a strange woman—*

Higgins had called Mendoza as soon as he got home, and told him about Rutland's funny little story. "The name just rang a bell in my head, and all of a sudden it hit me. Naudsinger. It was back in March, a homicide, I think it was Ocean View Avenue but you can look it up. That old-fashioned locket with the name engraved on it was part of the loot, so there's got to be some connection, Luis."

"That's a funny coincidence all right, George," said Mendoza. "I'll look it up in the morning and we'll see what shows. Did you hear the citizen's name?"

"It'll be in Rutland's report to the watch commander."

On Thursday morning Mendoza passed that on to Hackett and began to look in the files. "Hell," said Hackett, "I was on that, we never had a lead on it at all." They looked over the reports.

On March ninth a house on Ocean View Avenue had been burglarized. It belonged to a Mrs. Marian Cook, and she and her daughter had been away from home visiting another daughter in Bakersfield. But Ralph Naudsinger had been at home. He had rented a room from Mrs. Cook for nearly twenty years; he was a quiet old bachelor who drove a truck for a laundry; he'd been fifty-seven. The burglar had apparently thought the house was empty, broken in a back door, and been surprised to find Naudsinger there. By the evidence Naudsinger had put up a little fight, and ended up dead, knocked down against a heavy dining table. Mrs. Cook had said all her jewelry was missing, a miscellaneous collection not worth much, and the TV, a clock-radio, and a little cash, and Naudsinger had had a gold wristwatch and a ring with a diamond, also gone. The locket had been Mrs. Cook's, a family heirloom, the locket with the name engraved on it, Martha Deere.

62

"But what the hell," said Hackett, "so it ends up somewhere in a pawnshop in Hollywood, the burglar got rid of it, and somebody bought it."

"Well," said Mendoza, "it was a homicide after all. It's just worth following up, Art."

The night watch had left them two new heists, and everybody else was busy on those. They went up to Hollywood in the Ferrari and talked to the day-watch commander at Hollywood Division station, who remembered Rutland's report. He rummaged around and found the locket for them. It was an old-fashioned-looking thing, with ornate engraving of a flowery border and the name in intricate script. The address was for a Mrs. Quackenbush on Kingsley Drive.

"This is a goddamned waste of time," said Hackett.

"You know my hunches, Arturo. I think there's something off-beat here."

It was a block of mingled old single houses and apartments. The address was one of the houses, and the woman who answered the door was about thirty, plump, and plain, with suspicious eyes and protruding teeth. She stared at Hackett's badge and the locket he showed her. "Yes, that's what I gave to the officer yesterday. We don't want any part of anything like that. Well, I told the officer, this woman in the apartment next door, she gave it to my little girl Martha, and it's certainly not suitable for a child and I tried to give it back but she wouldn't take it. She's been making up to Martha ever since she's lived there, stopping to talk to her, Martha out playing, and calling her pet names and all, and I don't like it, she's no better than she should be by appearances, them having men in at night sometimes and both with dyed hair and all. I said to my husband, I'll bet maybe she stole that thing, but anyway I didn't want Martha to have anything of hers, and when she wouldn't take it back I just thought, hand it over to the police in case it was stolen."

"Who is the woman?" asked Mendoza. "She lives in the apartment next door?"

"That's right, ground floor this side. I don't know their names, this one just moved in a couple of months ago, with the other one.

63

They're neither of them any better than they should be, ask me, dyed blond hair and tight clothes and a lot of makeup." Her narrow mouth drew primly over the teeth. "I don't want to know either of them, don't know nothing about them."

"Now really, Luis," said Hackett on the sidewalk, "this is just nothing."

"Well, look a little further," said Mendoza. At the eight-unit apartment next door, they looked at the name slot at the left-hand ground-floor apartment, and it said *Pilger*. There was a manageress on the premises across the hall; Mendoza pushed the bell and a fat cheerful-looking woman opened the door.

"What on earth do the police want with Ruth Pilger?" she asked in surprise. "She's a perfectly respectable girl."

"We're trying to trace some stolen property," said Mendoza. "Do you know where she works?"

"Why, yes, it's the Silver Comb Beauty Salon on Glendale Avenue. They both do. Ruth's lived here about three years, she just took in another girl to live with her a couple of months ago, her name's Doreen something, she works there too."

As they got back into the Ferrari Hackett said, "Chasing the wild geese in this weather. You and your hunches."

The Silver Comb Beauty Salon was a modest shop in a block of stores on that old street. They aroused some mild sensation among the females, one waiting in the small anteroom, others in a big open space beyond with the usual appurtenances of basins and standard hair dryers. A tall buxom woman in a white smock came out to look at the badges, and said blankly, "What's Ruth done to get the cops after her?"

"Nothing that we know of," said Mendoza, "we'd just like to talk to her for a few minutes."

She went away and spoke to another white-smocked female, who came out to them. "What's this all about anyway—cops?"

"Miss Pilger?" said Mendoza.

"Yeah, that's me, what do the cops want?" She was about thirty, with platinum-blond hair and a good figure.

Mendoza showed her the locket. "Oh, that's Doreen's," she said. "Or it was. What about it?"

64

"Doreen who?"

"Doreen Riegel, she's right back there, you want to talk to her?"

"Yes, please," said Mendoza. She was eyeing them in frank approving appraisal of his dapper tailoring, the neat moustache and regular features, Hackett's impressive bulk.

"So I'll get her for you. I think she just finished with a customer."

When Doreen Riegel appeared, the waiting woman had been shepherded off by another operator, and they had the anteroom to themselves, with its plastic upholstered chairs and couch, the plastic table with the glass ashtray.

"Sit down, Miss Riegel," said Mendoza. He showed her the locket. "We understand you wanted to give this to the little girl living next door." She was platinum blond too, about the same age as the other girl, with a vapidly pretty round face and china-blue eyes. She didn't look nervous, only surprised.

"Well, yeah, I did. She's a real cute little kid, I just love kids, I'd like some of my own but Harry didn't want any and then we got divorced— But why are the cops interested?"

"Where did you get this?" asked Mendoza. He'd laid the locket on the table in front of her.

She didn't answer for a moment, and then asked cautiously, "Why do you want to know?"

"It seems to be stolen property," said Mendoza.

She looked astounded. "What? Well, I will be damned. Well, I don't know anything about it. Honest, I don't."

"Where did you get it?" asked Mendoza again.

She looked down at the floor, and now she wore an embarrassed expression. She said in a low voice, "I suppose I got to tell you about it, or you'll think I stole it. Well, I didn't. Exactly. I guess you could say it was pay if you call it that. I never stole anything in my life."

"Get to the point," said Hackett. "Where'd you come by it?"

She wouldn't look at either of them. She said miserably, "Listen, everybody has a run of bad luck sometimes, don't they? Back

65

there at the end of last year I was sure down on my luck. The place I'd been working closed up and I couldn't get another job. I looked and looked, but there are a lot of beauty operators around, see. I was just about broke, and you got to eat and pay the rent. I got to admit it, I'm ashamed of it, but I'd been doing some hustling to get the rent and groceries. I was living down on Second Street, and I'd picked up guys in a couple of bars down there. And this one night I picked up this guy and we went back to his pad because he had a bottle and I didn't have anything at my place. And, well, he ducked out on me. We'd both had a few as the night went on, you know how it goes, and I guess we both fell asleep, and when I woke up about seven o'clock he was gone. Tell you the truth, I don't think he meant to cheat me, he seemed like a nice guy, but he said he had to go to work early and maybe he just forgot he hadn't paid me the twenty-five. Well, I wasn't about to hang around till he got back, and I just looked to see if there was any money there. I wouldn't have taken any more than he owed me. I found a couple of ten-spots in a drawer and I took those, and that thing— I thought I could hock it for a few bucks. But it was that same day I met Ruth again. We worked at the same place once, up in Hollywood, I hadn't seen her in a couple of years, we always liked each other. And it was the same day I ran into her again at the employment agency. She was there for Mrs. Marcos, Mrs. Marcos owns this shop, and one of the operators had just quit. And Ruth said right off I could have the job, it was just like fate or something. And when she heard how tough I'd been having it she asked me to move in with her, the rent had gone up and she'd be glad to have somebody to split it with. So I did, and everything's been fine ever since. Yeah, I can tell you what day it was, it was March eleventh.''

Mendoza was suppressing laughter. ''Do you know the fellow's name?''

She said ashamedly, ''Just his first one. Fred. He never said his last one. But I can tell you where his pad was. It was an old apartment at the corner of Fifth and Hoover, he had the front apartment

66

on the left. And that thing"— she nodded at the locket—"I forgot I had it till just the other day. Like I say, I like kids, and that's a cute little kid next door. Her name's Martha and when I came across that the other day I just thought I'd give it to her."

"So thanks very much," said Mendoza. In the street outside he started to laugh. "Talk about fate—and coincidence! My God, what a funny little tangle, Art. Two days after the burglary and homicide, and Fred still had part of the loot. Let's go see if he's still there."

They stopped for lunch first. And heading in that direction, they found the house on Ocean View Avenue and talked to Mrs. Marian Cook. She identified the locket instantly. "Yes, that's the one the burglar took when he killed Ralph. It belonged to my grandmother, Martha Deere was her maiden name, it's a family heirloom, it's real old and solid gold." She was annoyed that they wouldn't give it back to her at once.

There was just one apartment building on that corner, ancient and shabby. Mendoza found a parking slot on the street a block up and they walked back. There was a manager on the premises, and Mendoza showed him the badge and asked for a Fred among the tenants.

"You mean Fred Snyder? He's the only Fred here. Why you asking about him, is he in cop trouble?"

"He could be. Does he have a job?"

"Yeah, he works at some gas station. I don't know which one."

"Which apartment is he in?" asked Hackett.

"Two-ten upstairs. What's it all about?"

"You may be hearing," said Mendoza. They started back to headquarters. "And we'll have to get statements from everybody concerned in this, and that'll take a little time. But what a beautiful example of Nemesis. I like it, it's reassuring to know that it's an orderly universe. And just because George wanted to get in a little shooting practice."

They stopped at R. and I. downstairs and in five minutes Phil Landers handed them the package on Fred Snyder. Mendoza looked at it and began to laugh again. Snyder had a record of two burglary convictions, and had just got out of Susanville last December; he was just off parole now.

"Just as well they're nearly all stupid so we catch up to them," said Hackett. "Of all the damn fool things, Luis. You had a hunch all right."

They went up to the office and Mendoza called Welfare and Rehab, got hold of Snyder's P.A. officer. He said, "I got him a job at a Union station on Sunset, he was still there the last time I saw him, but now he's off P.A. who can say how long he'll stay there? He's like most of them, doesn't like to work too hard at the regular job."

By then it was after two-thirty. They went up to that Union station and found him still on the job. He was a big hulking young fellow with bushy dark hair and hands like hams, and he looked at Hackett's badge and said in surprise, "What you want me for? I ain't been doin' nothin'."

"Let's go back to headquarters and talk about it," said Mendoza. He was still protesting as he crawled into the cramped rear seat of the Ferrari.

At the office they took him into one of the interrogation rooms and faced him across the little table. Mendoza laid the locket in front of him. "Remember this? It was part of the loot you took at that house on Ocean View last March ninth."

Snyder said woodenly, "I never saw that thing before in my life."

"Now that's funny," said Hackett gently. "Doreen Riegel found it in one of your drawers after you walked out without paying her for services rendered, a couple of days later. She can testify to that, it was in your possession. Why did you keep it? Or was the rest of the loot still there too?"

"I don't know what you're talkin' about," said Snyder.

"Come on," said Mendoza, "you're not as stupid as all that, Fred. The owner identifies it as one item the burglar took, and two days later Doreen found it in your drawer. That ties you right up to that job, you can see that. Two plus two. And so that ties you up to the rest of it."

Snyder wriggled on the hard small chair. His expression was sullen and angry. "Oh, for Christ's sake," he said. "For Christ's sake. All this while after—I'd nearly forgot about that damned job—it isn't fair the way things happen!" Now he was looking disgusted. "And I didn't get hardly any kind of haul at that place, only about forty bucks in cash and a little mess of jewelry and an old TV. And that damned guy put up a fight, I didn't think there was anybody in the house, it was all dark, and then he come at me out of nowhere—"

"So he did," said Mendoza pleasurably, "and you clobbered him."

"Why did you still have this thing?" asked Hackett. "And the rest of the haul maybe?"

"Oh, for Christ's sake," said Snyder. "The only damn fence I know was out of town."

Mendoza laughed. "So simple when you know. Did you know that you killed the fellow? He fractured his skull when you knocked him down against that table."

Snyder looked astonished. "He did? For Christ's sake, I never meant to kill nobody."

"So," said Hackett, "you'll be up for Murder Two, Fred. A little change for you. Right now you're going over to jail."

"Oh, for Christ's sake," said Snyder dispiritedly.

Mendoza would apply for the warrant while Hackett ferried Snyder over to the main jail. But he was still laughing over the inexorable working of Nemesis, and went out to tell the rest of the men about this one; they all got a kick out of it too.

The artist sitting in on the session with the Vasquez brothers had produced a sketch of the redhead which the victims said was a good one, her to the life. If it was, nobody had lied in describing her as one gorgeous chick. She had a heart-shaped face, a pert tip-tilted nose, a rosebud mouth, and big dark eyes. Unfortunately, the black-and-white sketch couldn't show the red hair, but they could imagine it; she wore it long and loose to the shoulders, and it was curly. The copies of that sketch were getting made up in the lab, and with any luck would be ready for distribution to all the squads by the change of Traffic shift at four o'clock today.

The witnesses to the latest heist last night had been in to make statements, and Grace, Galeano, and Landers were out on the legwork on those; they had turned up some suspects from Records. They didn't find any of them before the end of shift. The heat was still building and they'd all be glad to get home tonight.

But as they came drifting out past the switchboard, where Farrell was getting ready to close it down and switch over to Communications, he beckoned Mendoza violently; he was on the phone. He said into it, "Just a moment, sir, I'll connect you with the Lieutenant. It's something on Carpenter, Lieutenant, he says he knows him."

Mendoza snatched up the phone eagerly. "Lieutenant Mendoza. You know something about Jerome Carpenter? May I have your name?"

"I'm Frank Garcia. Yeah, I know that guy, only you haven't got his right name. His right name's Andy Dickinson."

"Are you sure about recognizing the photograph?" asked Mendoza sharply, feeling let down. The identification of Carpenter was definite.

"Sure I'm sure. I'd know that bastard in the dark," said Garcia. "I'd never have noticed that picture, I don't read much of the paper but the sports section, but the damned garbage disposal's on the fritz and I was wrapping the garbage to take out to the trash, and I saw it. It says the cops want him for homicide, and there's this number to call. So I called. I'd like to help you get him but I don't see how."

"How long have you known him? Do you know where he's living?"

"No, not now I don't. Up to the last week I understand he was in a hotel room, the California Hotel on Santa Monica here in Hollywood, but of course that was the first place I looked and he'd checked out."

"Why were you looking for him?" asked Mendoza. The rest of the men were still hanging around to find out if they were going to get a lead on Carpenter.

"Well, for the love of God," said Garcia exasperatedly, "he's just run off with my wife, that's why. I've got to say we hadn't been getting along so good, Maria'd been nagging me about this and that, but I never thought she'd do anything like that, it was a big damn surprise when I came home last Friday and found she'd run off with this bastard. She leaves me a note, she says she's fed up with me and my lousy low-pay job and Andy's a lot more fun and a better spender, goodbye. Like I said, I went to that hotel but they weren't there, he'd checked out. I don't know where they are."

"Where did you meet him?" asked Mendoza.

"At one of the card rooms down in Gardena, about a month ago. Maria and me, we both like a friendly game, no big stakes, I can't afford it, I just work at a Sears store in the men's department. We got talking to him over a drink, and he's a pretty good-looking bastard, and he'd been doing all right sitting in at one of the poker tables. We ran into him there a few more times. He said he's just out of the Army, and he hadn't decided what he wanted to do yet, what kind of job to go for. He said he'd got himself a good stake and had time to look around. I guess that kind of impressed Maria."

"Do you know what car he's driving?"

"I've got to say no, except he's got one. Goddamn it, now I can guess that while I was at work like the honest citizen, him and Maria have been getting all cozied up together, me the innocent never suspecting a damned thing."

"Did he say where he got the stake?" asked Mendoza.

"Yeah, he'd been over in Vegas and got hot at poker."

"Well, is that all you can tell us? Has your wife got a car?"

"No, who can afford to run two cars on my salary?"

"Has she any relatives around here?"

"Yeah, her mother and her sister. But I've talked to them, naturally, she's always going shopping or to lunch with them and I thought she might be in touch. But she hasn't been. They're both mad at her for running out on me too." He passed over the names and addresses. "Not that I think it'll do you any good, but I suppose it's possible she might contact them sometime."

"Was he registered at the hotel as Dickinson?"

"Well, yeah, of course, that's his name."

"It's not his right name," said Mendoza dryly. "We know that."

"Is that so?" said Garcia. "But I know it's his real name, I saw it on his Social Security card."

"What?" said Mendoza.

"Yeah, it was one night at the card room, he bought a round of drinks and he put his billfold on the table and it was open to where he had his Social Security card, I just happened to glance at it."

"Well, I will be damned," said Mendoza. "*¿Qué es esto?* Thanks very much for calling in, Garcia. You may have given us a little help at that."

"I hope you catch up to the bastard," said Garcia. "Not that it'd get me my wife back. But on the other hand, if you put him in jail she'll have to come back, she's got no money of her own. And I haven't decided if I'd want her back at that."

Mendoza thanked him again and passed the gist of that on. "Gardena," said Hackett thoughtfully.

"*Pues sí*," said Mendoza. "The gambling dens. If Carpenter's a gambler, he won't be able to stay away from the cards." There was a time when Luis Rodolfo Vicente Mendoza had been a hot poker player too; the domesticities had ruined his game, but the gamblers he knew all too well. "And by all the evidence he doesn't know this town well—that's the only place he could get in a legal game."

Palliser said grimly, "Get some copies of that shot made up and spread them around all those card rooms. Get them out to every squad on that beat." The squads would be out of Seventy-seventh Street Division.

"I'm ahead of you," said Mendoza. "Rory, get me the lab." And it was half-past six, but they didn't grudge the delay if it was going to give them a line on Carpenter. Mendoza got Duke, just in

72

to the night watch at the lab, and told him what they wanted. If they got right on it, the lab could get all those prints made up overnight, for distribution around tomorrow.

"But I wonder," said Galeano, "where the hell he came by that Social Security card? Who's Andy Dickinson?"

"And echo answers," said Mendoza. "It might be worth asking about, Nick. But where's to ask? We wouldn't get an answer out of the government before next Christmas."

He got home nearly an hour late, ready to apologize to his household. In the kitchen Mairí shook her tight silver curls at him. "We didna wait for you on dinner, but I've something warm in the oven for you."

"Fine," said Mendoza, and reached to the cupboard to pour himself a drink. The alcoholic half-Siamese, El Señor, could hear that cupboard opened the length of the house away, and came at a run begging for his share of rye. Mendoza poured him half an ounce in a saucer, and went down the hall to find the rest of the family congregated in the living room—the other three cats Bast, Sheba and Nefertite, Cedric, the Old English sheepdog, Alison and the twins, baby Luisa on Alison's lap tugging at her hair.

Johnny and Teresa pounced on him. "Daddy, Daddy, we're goin' to a pool party!" yelled Johnny exuberantly.

"It's on Sunday at Carla's house—a pool party!" contributed Terry, jumping up and down.

Mendoza looked at Alison blankly. "Don't you think they're a little young to take up billiards, *querida*?"

Alison burst out laughing. "A swimming-pool party, *estúpido*. It was a Mrs. Coatesworth called just a few minutes ago, she's having some of their friends' children over, she said since Terry and Carla had made friends this semester she thought she'd ask the twins. She's having the mothers too. They live in Burbank. Celebrate school being out, it's very nice of her."

"Carla's my bestest friend at school," said Terry devotedly.

And as Alison was always saying, her Scots Presbyterian father would be turning in his grave over the parochial school, but at least

73

they'd get a better foundation. "We'll have to go shopping tomorrow and get you a bathing suit," said Alison, "and some trunks for Johnny."

"I want a green bathing suit!"

"I don't care what color." Johnny was scornful of vain females.

"Very nice." Mendoza sat down with his drink.

"So what delayed you?" she asked.

He started to tell her, and Mairí came in to shepherd the twins up to their baths. "You can lay out the man's dinner for him, *achara*, and I'll take the baby too, it's past time she was in bed. Off you go now, you two." The twins vanished noisily up the stairs, still shouting about the party.

The night watch sat around until nine-thirty with nothing happening. Then Communications relayed a call from a squad, and Conway and Piggott took it. When they got there, Conway said, "Oh-oh, here we are again."

It was an all-night station on Beverly, and the Traffic man confirmed that it had been Jack the Stripper again. The attendant was an elderly fat man, and he was furious and embarrassed. Some of these attendants had been college kids earning the extra money, but some of the retired men took this kind of job to supplement the pension. This one's name was Trapp, and he said, "I just thank God that girl wasn't still here, my God, I'd of died. My wife keeps after me to go on a diet." He had a big fat stomach and narrow shoulders, and standing there naked, he was hardly an Adonis. "The girl, thank God she'd just left. Come bumping in here on a flat tire, she didn't know how to change it. Lucky it only happened up in the next block. I'd just put the spare on for her and she like to have kissed me, she gave me a five-buck tip. She'd just pulled out when that damn guy drove in—" They had heard the tale before: the Stripper following back to the garage ostensibly to pay for the gas, pulling the gun, ordering the victim to strip, and walking off with his clothes so he couldn't go back to the street to get the plate number. It was the same description: about five-ten, dark blond, a young fellow about twenty-five.

74

"How'm I goin' to get home?" asked Trapp plaintively. "It'll be broad daylight when the owner gets here and my wife can't drive." In the end they drove up to his apartment and got some clothes for him.

"But it's sort of gone beyond a joke," said Piggott on the way back to the office. "He's hit about seven times since the first of the year, and there's no line on him at all." About all they could do on it, as they had on the others, was to take Trapp's statement and file it away.

The lab had got busy overnight and all those prints of the blown-up photos of Jerome Carpenter were ready by the time the day men came on, for the distribution around. Galeano was off on Friday, but most of the rest of them started out on that to save time. There were a lot of card parlors down in Gardena, the only incorporated town in the county where the card parlors were legal.

Mendoza, Palliser, Calhoun, and Grace spent a good part of the day covering those places, handing over the prints, asking cooperation: If anybody should spot Carpenter, please call in. Most of the proprietors were cooperative; a few of them weren't too fond of cops and said sure, sure, but they could suspect that the minute they went out the print would be tossed in the trash bin. But it was the best handle they'd had on Carpenter so far. The domestic life had ruined Mendoza's poker game, but he'd been a Vice cop before he got sent up to Robbery-Homicide and the gamblers he knew, they couldn't stay away from the tables. And there were more cooperative proprietors than the other kind.

Hackett took a batch of the prints over to Seventy-seventh Street Division and talked to a Lieutenant Quigley at Robbery-Homicide there. Quigley was stocky and bald, probably nearing retirement. "Damn it," he said, "I hope this helps you lay hands on him, Sergeant. That patrolman, getting it just for nothing. These goddamned punks roving around." Gunther's funeral was scheduled for this afternoon, and there'd be a lot of L.A.P.D. men attending it, the Chief making a speech. "But we can't hand these out to the squads until the shift changes at four o'clock now."

"I know, I know," said Hackett, "but it could be the best lead we've got."

"Well, we'll be on it. By the way, how are you boys getting on with Pat Calhoun up there?"

"Oh, fine," said Hackett. "Just fine. He's a good boy."

Quigley grinned. "Just don't underestimate him. He's also a smart boy."

They couldn't just forget about the rest of the work on hand, and Landers and Higgins had gone out looking for the possible heisters. They only found one of them, Alfredo Reyes, to bring in for questioning. He had the right record for it and he conformed to the description given by the witnesses, but there wasn't any solid evidence on him. He didn't have an alibi, but he didn't show any signs of coming apart and admitting the job; there wasn't enough to charge him on, and they let him go.

The other men came trailing in along toward the end of the shift, and everybody was tired; it had been a grueling day out on the street in ninety-eight-degree heat. But at five-thirty a new call went down, to a homicide.

Mendoza said, "*¡Por Dios!* The night watch'll be here in half an hour."

Calhoun stabbed out his cigarette and got up. "I don't mind taking a preliminary look." He cocked his head at Wanda. "Care to come along, beautiful? You're so hot on getting street experience."

"For heaven's sake," said Wanda, "if you're so eager for overtime, I'm not. I've got an appointment to have my hair done at seven o'clock, and by the time I get home I'll be starving." Calhoun laughed and went out.

"And the night customers will be drifting in to all those gambling dens," said Mendoza. "Keep your fingers crossed that somebody spots Carpenter, *compadres.*"

The address for the new body was Vendome Street, and the patrolman waiting for detectives was Carlson. It was a small duplex,

76

needing paint, with brown grass in front. "So what's the story?" asked Calhoun.

"That's up to you," said Carlson. "Man says he came home from work and found his wife dead. Looks as if she's been strangled. His name's Samuel Tucker."

He was a nondescript man about thirty, medium size, with dark hair and a lantern jaw. He was sitting in a chair in the living room, which held some shabby old furniture, with his head in his hands. Calhoun asked him some questions, and he answered in a dull voice. "I dunno what happened. I just come home from work and found her like that. I come home about five maybe."

Conway took a look at the body. It was on the bed in the front bedroom, and even if she'd been strangled he could see that she'd been a good-looking female, with long dark hair and a luscious figure, readily visible since she was stark naked. He told Carlson to call the lab. "Where do you work, Mr. Tucker?"

"I'm on the maintenance crew at a public school up on Union Street. We all left at four, usual time, and Pete and me stopped to have a couple of beers at a bar on Third, like we usually do. Denny, he don't drink, he headed straight home, and I guess I got here about five, and there she was—I dunno what happened."

At six-thirty Rich Conway showed up and Calhoun passed all that on. "Well, the lab may turn up something," said Conway.

"Anyway, it's all yours." Calhoun went back to his car. He was rather sorry that Conway was on night watch. He felt that they might get to be good friends, they were the same kind—with an eye for the girls, and playing the field.

C h a p t e r 5

Conway saw the lab men, Duke and Cheney, start to work getting photographs and beginning to dust the place, and talked to Tucker, who just kept saying he didn't know anything about it. He'd been at work, he'd come home and found his wife dead. She was twenty-four and her name was Gladys. Tomorrow somebody would have to look up the maintenance crew at that school and get his alibi pinned down for the record.

After the morgue wagon had come and gone, Conway went over to the other half of the duplex. The tenants there were a Mr. and Mrs. Hess. They were middle-aged, he a weedy thin man and she scraggly and gray-haired.

"Something happened next door?" she asked, looking at the badge. "Police coming, we saw the patrol car come up and I said to Henry, that woman bringing down police on us, it's disgraceful. What happened?"

Conway told them and they were horrified and fascinated. "Murdered!" she said. "Well, all I can say is, she brought it on herself, and serve her right, though we shouldn't speak ill of the dead."

"And why do you say that?" asked Conway.

She said righteously, "Well, I don't like to talk about such nastiness even to the police," and she was eyeing Conway's good looks and well-tailored suit a little suspiciously—"but that girl was just no good, a real bad girl, she brought men home with her nearly every day, and her with a decent husband off at work like an honest man, it was disgraceful. She must have known I saw it, she just didn't care.''

Hess said, ''They moved in here about six months ago, and inside a week we could tell the kind she was, I didn't see it, I'm at work, but Ada's home most of the time and she says the girl didn't even try to cover it up. We don't know anything but their names, this place is owned by a realty company and they arrange for somebody to cut the grass once in a while, and like that, we got no reason to talk to the people on the other side. I don't think we ever exchanged a word with either of them.''

''And when I saw what kind she was I didn't want to,'' said the woman. ''A real brazen one she was, she'd go off every day about noon, all got up in flashy clothes and makeup, and pretty soon she'd come back with some man and naturally I could guess what they were up to over there. It was a disgrace, and her poor husband not suspecting a thing.''

''Was there a man there today?'' asked Conway.

She nodded. ''That there was. I saw them come back, it was about one o'clock. She doesn't have a car but she came back in a car with a man. I'd seen him before, it wasn't the first time he'd come back with her. But there were others too, different men, most every day.''

''What about this one?'' asked Conway. ''Can you describe him?''

''Well, about all I can tell you, he was kind of big and had dark hair, ordinary clothes.''

''What about the car?''

''Oh, I don't know what it was, a sedan of some kind. And he was there about two hours—disgraceful—I happened to be out on the porch to see if the mail had come, and saw him drive off, it was just three o'clock.''

''Did you see her then?''

''No, I just saw him drive away.''

''Do you know where she went to meet the men?''

She said indignantly, "And how would I know that, I'm a decent woman and don't know how one like that might do to take up with strange men. All I know is, she'd go off nearly every day about noon or a little before all dressed up, up toward the main streets one way or the other, and usually came back with some man in a car. Different men."

Conway said, "We'll want statements from you, there'll be other detectives talking to you tomorrow."

"That's all right," said Hess. "Whatever we can do to help the police."

Conway stood on the narrow sidewalk and ruminated. All the boyfriends, he thought. And that rather sounded as if most of them might have been casual pickups—the wife earning a little money on the side? If they'd been previously known to her, why had she left home to meet them? The dates could have been set up by phone. And she'd been on foot. Of course she could have taken a bus on either of the main drags, Beverly or Third, but by what the Hess woman said, she hadn't usually been gone long. Going off about noon, and today she'd come home at one. With a man who'd been there before. There were bars and restaurants on both main drags. She could have met the man anywhere, casually or by appointment, and either way it was going to be a headache for the day men to work.

On the other side of the duplex the lab men were still at work. Tucker was sitting in a sagging armchair with his head in his hands. Conway eyed him with abstract sympathy. Poor devil married to a girl like that, they did say the husband was always the last to know. He asked, "Can I have the names of the men you work with?"

"Sure," said Tucker listlessly. "Pete Lacey and Denny Rios. We was at work together all day like usual. It's the elementary school over on Union. We're off at four, but Pete and me stopped to have a couple of beers so I didn't get home till about five or a little after."

"I guess that's all for right now," said Conway. "The other detectives will probably want to talk to you again."

"Sure," said Tucker dully. "Sure, that's all right."

Conway went back to the office and told Schenke and Piggott about it, started to type a report. The day men could take it from here.

On Saturday morning Mendoza read over the night report, passed it around; only that new homicide had turned up, and Conway's report was suggestive. Higgins said, "The girl was making it hot and heavy with a succession of boyfriends, possibly the pickups. Possibly at bars on either of the main drags. I suppose we go and ask. More to the point, did the husband know about it?"

Palliser stroked his handsome straight nose and said, "Yes. And if anybody remembers her picking up the men would they know any names, George? The damn-fool woman was asking for trouble, and she found it. And I don't suppose any of those bars will be open until around eleven."

It was Landers' day off. There were still the heists to work and nowhere to go on the latest hit by Jack the Stripper. Time would tell as to whether the artist's sketch would turn up the gorgeous redhead and her partner, or whether the photographs would turn up Carpenter. Toward noon an autopsy report came in, on the Dunlaps. As expected, they had both died of the overdose of Demerol, and the doctors thought they had been dead for a month or six weeks. "*Por Dios,*" said Mendoza to himself. The things people did to each other.

He was just about to leave for an early lunch when Farrell rang him and said, "I've got a call from Kansas City for you, it's about the werewolf."

"*Cómo,*" said Mendoza. "Hold it one second." He went to look in the communal office. Higgins, Hackett, and Galeano were in and he beckoned them urgently back to his office, told Farrell to put through the call, and punched the amplifier. The voice boomed out into the room, a deep baritone. "This is Lieutenant Gearhart, Kansas City Homicide Bureau, I'm calling about this thing on the N.C.I.C. wire, like I told the sergeant."

"Lieutenant Mendoza here, so what have you got to tell us?"

"Well, we get kind of busy here sometimes and I just looked over the current bulletin this morning and saw what you boys are asking about. These damned lunatic mutilation killings. By all the M.O. and the details of the mutilations, we had that one operating here since about two years ago."

"*De veras,*" said Mendoza softly. "We said he hadn't just had the urge recently. What's your end of it?"

"I can look up the names and dates if you want," said Gearhart, "but the details I remember all too well, I was heading the investigation. Altogether there were twenty of them, Mendoza—twenty hookers tied up and tortured and killed."

"*¡Dios millón demonios desde infierno!*" said Mendoza.

"And there was that same trademark you mentioned, the cross carved between the breasts. Twenty, my God, from about two years ago up till last December. The last one was December twenty-third, my wife was mad because I got called away from a Christmas party."

"God Almighty," said Hackett.

"There just wasn't any line on the lunatic," said Gearhart. "We asked the head-doctors for any educated guesses—"

"And I know what you heard," said Mendoza. "He could look as sane as anybody."

"And he's evidently not lunatic enough that he doesn't cover his tracks. Of course anybody can pick up the hooker, get taken home with her. They were all killed in their own places, and by what our lab got we deduced that he stripped to do the actual torture and mutilation, and he must have got pretty damn well covered with blood in the process, but it looked as if he'd cleaned himself up in the bathroom afterward, bloodstained towels left around, so he could walk out clean as a whistle."

"On the nose," said Mendoza. "That's our werewolf."

"And that's the hell of a good name for him," said Gearhart grimly. "I tell you, we nearly lost our minds on it. There wasn't a single lead. All of a sudden, there'd be another one, and my God, you know the hookers, nobody noticing which particular john they picked up when or where. And he wasn't particular, Mendoza.

One of them was a sixteen-year-old, hustling to support a habit, and another was fifty-two and a raddled old lush, for God's sake.''

"He took them because they were available,'' said Mendoza.

"That looks about the size of it,'' said Gearhart. "It's got to be the same boy, by the M.O. The werewolf. The last one was last December like I say. Then, no more. When we hadn't had another by February we began to hope he'd left town.''

"Which he had,'' said Mendoza with a mirthless laugh. "He moved on here. I wonder why. He killed the first one here on April thirtieth.''

"Well, I can only wish you luck in hunting him,'' said Gearhart, "and going by our experience you'll damn well need it. He's a ghost. Oh, I forgot to say we got just one thing, but it won't help you any. On one of them, we got a witness, another hooker, who saw the girl who got killed leave the bar with him. It had to have been him, that was about nine in the evening and the autopsy report said she died about eleven. God, those girls must have gone through the tortures of the damned—cheap hookers, but they were human beings after all. The girl couldn't describe him, the place was dark as hell, you know the bars, but she told us one thing. She said he was carrying a little bag. She was across the room, she couldn't give us any idea about his size or age or looks, but she said he had a bag, like a briefcase.''

"*¡Vaya!*'' said Mendoza. "With his tools in it, maybe. All the nice sharp tools he needs to gratify the bloodlust? Now that's a thing.''

"I had the same idea,'' said Gearhart. "What was done to those women, he'd need the tools—several of them, the doctors thought something like a cleaver to cut off the heads, and at least a couple of different knives for the rest of it.''

"We heard the same from our doctors.''

"Well, that's every last thing I can tell you. He was here, and he left, and now you've got him.''

"I only wish to God we had,'' said Mendoza. "But thanks for calling.''

"I'm just sorry we can't offer you any more help," said Gearhart.

Mendoza put down the phone. "I had the feeling this wasn't the werewolf's first time out."

"My God," said Higgins. "Twenty! It'd figure out to a little less than one a month, Luis. My God."

"Back in K.C.," said Mendoza. "And here he's been doing better than that, hasn't he? Five in seven weeks, *por Dios*. It could be we'll get another any day."

"Good God," said Higgins, "and ghost is another word for him, there's just no handle at all. He could be any man in the county."

"I don't know," said Mendoza meditatively. "It's a big county. There are the available hookers in most places in the county, but all five have been on our beat. That says to me that he lives or works somewhere right downtown."

"And that takes in a damn big area too," said Galeano. "It wouldn't narrow it down much."

"Unfortunately no," said Mendoza. "Well—" He brushed his moustache and stood up. "Let's go and have lunch. There's not one damn thing we can do about it at the moment."

Palliser and Grace had gone out on a first cast on the new homicide, the Tucker girl. They had tried the nearest couple of bars on Beverly, and got a little from both bartenders.

"Listen," said the first bartender, "this is a respectable place, we don't let the B-girls in here, but what can I say to an ordinary customer who just happens to get talking to another customer? They're not doing anything I can object to, and how the hell do I know what they're going to do if they walk out together? And at that it was only a couple of times. Yeah, that dame I know, Gladys her name is, I heard one guy call her that. Good-looker about twenty-five, dark hair and a nice figure. The funny thing is, I don't think she was peddling it, she just likes the fellows, was a free and easy dame. She'd be in here maybe a couple of times a week, and most times she'd meet a guy here, I mean he'd be waiting for her, they knew each other, and once or twice she got talking to a guy and they went out together but I couldn't prove she hadn't known him before, I just had the feeling. You know?"

"Do you know any of their names?" asked Palliser.

"Now how would I? They're just customers. We get some regulars in from the office buildings around, we've got a nice line of fancy sandwiches and some of the men work around here drop in regular for lunch, but I just know their faces, not their names." There was a waitress, who told them the same thing.

They started up the street for another place in the next block. It was close to a hundred again today. "Just a free and easy dame," said Grace, his chocolate-brown face wearing a slightly amused expression. "But why should one of the casual boyfriends have killed her? The report said she'd probably been strangled."

"God knows," said Palliser. "Anything could have triggered it, Jase. They got into an argument and he lost his temper."

At the next place the bartender had recognized the name, and told them a little more of the same. Like the other places along here, this one had regular lunch customers from the offices nearby, but he'd never seen that girl try to pick up one of those. The couple of men she'd got talking to, gone out with, had been casual customers, and most of the time she'd had a fellow waiting for her, somebody she knew. Different fellows, and of course he didn't know any of their names.

They decided to have an early lunch there, and while they waited for it over coffee Palliser said, "The picture emerges a little clearer. She didn't often actually pick up the strangers. She just had a lot of boyfriends, acquired either before or after she got married. She'd meet them and they'd buy her lunch, a couple of drinks, and then they'd take her home for a roll in the hay. And apparently she didn't give a damn that the neighbors would be bound to see her with all the different men. Funny in a way, though God knows there are enough of that kind around."

"I wonder if the husband suspected anything?" said Grace. "You'd have thought she'd have been nervous that the neighbors might tell him."

"By the report, they didn't socialize, didn't know each other, and the husband's usually the last to know. God, doing the legwork in this weather—" At least all of these places were air-conditioned. "But I suppose there's just a chance we might locate whatever place she was in yesterday, and somebody might know the man." She hadn't been at either of these first two places yesterday.

They started out again at one-thirty and tried a third bar and grill a couple of blocks up.

The autopsy report came in on that Edward Jackson, the parking lot attendant, and Wanda glanced over it. He had died of a coronary. She had found the office deserted when she came back from lunch, but half an hour later Calhoun brought in a possible suspect and said, "I need a witness to sit in on the questioning. Where is everybody?"

"Haven't you taken it in yet that I'm a detective too?" asked Wanda. "Really, Pat, I'm not just a glorified secretary."

He grinned at her. "I'm not used to working with the beautiful blond females on the job. All right, you can sit in, but I warn you he's been cussing a blue streak."

The suspect went on cussing and calling them names. He conformed to the description given by the two witnesses and it was a fairly distinctive one, he had long sideburns and a moustache longer than usual. His name was Juan Diaz, and he had a pedigree of two counts of armed robbery. He didn't have an alibi for the time in question, and after they'd talked to him awhile they both thought it was worth the trouble of arranging a lineup, to see if the witnesses could identify him. They could hold him for twenty-four hours without a charge. Arrange the lineup for tomorrow morning and see what came of it. Calhoun took him over to the jail. He was still cussing, and he had a colorful vocabulary.

After lunch Higgins went out on some of the necessary spadework on the new one, checking that Tucker's alibi. Tucker could give them Pete Lacey's address, if only the street name, Lexington in Hollywood, and he was in the phone book. But Tucker didn't have any idea where Denny Rios lived except that it was somewhere in Hollywood too, and there were several duplicate names in the phone book. Neither of the men would be at work on Saturday. Higgins went hunting Rios first and landed the right one on the third try. It was Fernwood Place, a small apartment building. Rios was a big dark fellow about forty, and he answered Higgins' questions readily. He was shocked to hear about Tucker's wife. "Murdered?" he said incredulously. "My God, that's awful, she was just a young woman. I suppose one of these creeps stoned on dope or liquor breaking in."

"We don't know yet," said Higgins. "All I want to know is, was Tucker at work all day yesterday?"

Rios looked surprised. "Well, sure he was. You wouldn't be thinking Sam would hurt her? That's just crazy. I never met her but I know Sam was pretty crazy about her, they just got married last year. But sure, he was at the school all day, we're on eight to four. We all left together at four o'clock, and Sam and Pete were going to stop somewhere to have a couple of beers. I don't drink and besides I had to pick up my wife at five, she works at a coffee shop uptown and she doesn't have a car."

By Conway's report the woman had been dead for at least a couple of hours before the police had first seen her; the body had been cold. Higgins thanked him and went to see if Pete Lacey was at home. He was about Tucker's age, tall and bony with sparse blond hair, and he said the same things, hearing about the murder. "Oh, that'll be real bad for Sam, he was nuts about that girl, I know. They'd only been married about a year. Sure, he was at work all day, same as usual, our regular hours. All of us came out to the parking lot together at four o'clock, and Sam and I stopped for a couple of beers at a place on Alvarado. We don't do that every day, but more often than not. In this damned hot weather a beer tastes good. I guess we'd of got there about a quarter past four, and we were there maybe half an hour, at least Sam was. We had two beers apiece and he left about a quarter, ten of five, that's right close to where he lives and he'd probably of got home by five or a little after. I stayed on and had another beer, I'm not married and it don't matter what time I get home."

So that was that, thought Higgins, starting back to the office. Whoever had strangled the woman it hadn't been Tucker. If they could somehow locate whatever man had come home with her yesterday, that was probably the answer.

Palliser and Grace were hitting some paydirt a little later in the day. This was the fifth bar and grill they had tried, a place on Third Street, talking to the bartenders. This one recognized Gladys Tucker's description, hadn't known her name. He said she had come in once or twice a week, and met a boyfriend for lunch. "Different boyfriends," he said with a leer. "I guess I'd seen her meet up with four or five different men. Different times. They'd have lunch and leave together. Well, for God's sake, no, I never got the idea she was on the make. Just, she had a lot of different boyfriends. That's all I know about her, why are the cops asking?"

They didn't waste time telling him. "Was she in here yesterday?" asked Palliser.

"Well, yeah, as a matter of fact she was," said the bartender. "She came in about noon, and one of the boyfriends was waiting for her and they had a couple of drinks and some sandwiches, and they left about one or one-fifteen."

"Had she met the same man here before? Can you describe him?"

"Well, yeah, she had, five or six times before. Well, he's a big husky guy about thirty, all I can say. No, I never heard her say his name. But one thing I can tell you, he comes in here for early dinner maybe three, four times a week. Sometime like about four-thirty." Like the others, this place served meals, and there was a waiter. The bartender beckoned him over; he was a young Latin type with a hairline moustache. "You know this guy, Tony, he's about six feet and husky, with a kind of long face and long nose, he's come in quite a few times for dinner, real early. And he'd meet this girl for drinks and lunch, good-looking dark girl with a real nice figure."

"Oh, yeah, I think I know the one you mean," said Tony. "They were here for lunch yesterday."

"You know anything about him?" asked the bartender. "I don't know why in hell the cops are interested but they are."

Tony looked at Palliser and Grace curiously. "Is that so?" he said. "You're cops? That's funny, because I thought he was a cop."

"What?" said Palliser.

"Yeah"— Tony looked at the bartender. "You wouldn't have noticed, it was your day off, it was last Sunday, that guy came in later than usual for dinner, and he had a blue uniform on and he was packing a gun in a belt holster. When I brought him his coffee I asked if he was a cop, and he laughed and said no, just a security guard. He said he was a night security guard up at the old Goldwyn Studios in Hollywood."

"Jackpot!" said Grace. "The legwork does sometimes pay off, John."

Mendoza was alone in the office at four o'clock, swiveled around in his desk chair staring out the window, when Farrell rang him and said, "This time it's Boston, Lieutenant. A Captain Prothero."

"Put him through," said Mendoza tersely.

Prothero had a rather nasal deep voice. "The sergeant said you're Lieutenant Mendoza? It's this thing on the N.C.I.C. wire, I just spotted it today, or rather Sergeant Murphy did and brought it in to me. We've been doing the overtime on a double homicide, this is the first chance I've had to call L.A. This lunatic killing and mutilating all the prostitutes."

"Yes," said Mendoza. "Do you know something about it?"

"Not a damn thing," said Prothero crisply, "except that we had him first. I looked up the dates, and he started his bloody operations here nearly four years ago, call it three years and eight months back."

"Oh, now, you don't tell me," said Mendoza softly. "Up to when?"

"Just two years ago," said Prothero. "It's got to be the same lunatic, there are all the same trademarks. The decapitation, the cross carved between the breasts, and they were all hookers in business for themselves."

"Tell me the bad news—how many?"

And Prothero said, "Over eighteen months, sixteen," and Mendoza let out a long breath. "All the trademarks you had on the hot line—by what our lab figured, he stripped to do the actual bloody work, and cleaned up in the bathroom when he'd done it. The doctors said there wasn't any expert anatomical knowledge."

"That's what we've heard. The different tools used, maybe a cleaver, a couple of serrated knives."

"None of the women were what you'd classify as high-class hookers, and they were all ages."

"He's not particular," said Mendoza. "Just the available women."

"That's right," said Prothero. "And we didn't have one single damned lead on him. We went around on it, you can imagine. Sixteen, my God. And just nowhere to go on it worth a damn. The lab picked up a few latents, but they weren't on file. He just picked the women up, killed them, and vanished into the dark. You know the kind of dives the hookers haunt, and he may have picked some of them off the street in nice weather. Nobody saw any of the victims pick up the john on the relevant dates. There was nothing we could do about it but take the statements and read the lab reports and file them away."

"That's what we're doing," said Mendoza. "You'll be interested to know that when he left your territory he moved on to Kansas City. That was apparently just after his last operation with you. He did twenty there."

"Twenty!" Prothero was shaken and horrified. "Oh, my God!"

"Those boys went around on it too, and it was the same thing, no leads, nowhere to start looking. Then all of a sudden, no more dead hookers. They had the last one back in December. He then arrived here, we don't know when but he pulled the first one here on April thirtieth, and there have been four since."

"Oh, my good Christ in heaven!" said Prothero. "That's forty-one! Forty-one!"

"Well, it's not a record," said Mendoza. "Some of the classic mass killers have topped that. And I wonder if somebody else is going to call me from New York or Miami or Seattle to tell me how many he accounted for there."

"My good Christ!" said Prothero. "And I've covered some messy homicides in my time but those were the bloodiest. What those poor damned females went through—the tortures of the damned before they finally died. I can't offer you any suggestions on it, but you know that. I hope to hell his luck runs out and you can spot him."

"And that may be our only hope of catching up," said Mendoza, "if he slips up—or Nemesis takes after him. One thing I will say, Prothero. I'm not a head-doctor but I can deduce this and that from the history we've now got on him. He's getting the urge oftener, and up to now he's evidently been able to stay looking sane on the surface, functioning normally, probably working at jobs to earn a living, not arousing any suspicions that there's anything wrong with him. But he's getting the urge oftener, and that could say that his grip on reality is giving way. One of these days or nights he could go right over the edge, do something to bring suspicion down on himself, give himself away somehow."

"That could be," said Prothero. "I hope to God he does."

"It may be the only way of getting him," repeated Mendoza. As he put the phone down Hackett came in and he told him about all that.

"Forty-one!" said Hackett incredulously. "But my God, Luis—"

"I'll tell you, Art, I just don't see one like this going on forever maintaining the sane front. Sooner or later he'll drop right over the edge. Start foaming at the mouth or throwing fits or something, and at least get tucked away even if we never hear about it, know it was him responsible for the dead hookers."

"I'll agree with that," said Hackett soberly. "And if he does, he just might start talking about it at the top of his voice—they often do—and we would hear about it."

"*Claro que sí.* All we can do is wait," said Mendoza.

And Hackett said, "He's about due to hit again if we're deducing right."

They both sat in silence for a while, thinking about those women horribly dead, and then the phone rang on Mendoza's desk.

Farrell said, "I've now got one of the house dicks at the Hyatt on Flower. He says he knows something about those bank heisters."

"So put him on," said Mendoza.

The voice at the other end was measured and leisurely. "You've got these bank heisters on the N.C.I.C. hot line. Roger Price and Arnold Unger. I just happened to notice it an hour ago. I thought you'd like to know where they are."

"Can I have your name, please? You know where they are?"

"That I do. I'm Howard Anderson, and I'm one of the house detectives at the Hyatt on Flower Street, but I didn't get born that way. Up to two years ago I was Captain on the Santa Monica Department, when I retired. Twenty-seven years in, Lieutenant. And fate is a very funny thing. Naturally, being out of service I don't see the N.C.I.C. bulletins regular, but I've still got some buddies down at headquarters there and once in a while I drop in for a chat about what's going on. I was down there this afternoon, I don't come on duty here till five, and I just happened to see the current bulletin on Sergeant Delgado's desk. And there was the want on Price and Unger. It gave me a little jolt. I figured it'd be just as quick to call you from the hotel. Just as it happens I was the one put the arm on Price for another job about six years back, which is why I recognized him. Unger I don't know, but he's probably the guy with him."

"You know where they are?" asked Mendoza.

"You bet," said Anderson amusedly. "I recognized Price but of course I didn't know he was wanted for anything until I saw the bulletin. He and the other guy, they're in an expensive suite right here at the hotel, with a couple of damned good-looking girls, and they've been living it up in a big way—room service, champagne, having a high old time.''

Mendoza began to laugh. ''My God, the typical pros, can't think twenty-four hours ahead! *Gracias, amigo,* we'll be over to get them pronto.'' He called the local FBI office and got Gerber just as he was leaving.

Gerber swore. ''Damn it, I'm supposed to take my wife out to dinner tonight. All right, all right, I'll meet you there.''

Mendoza and Hackett called their respective wives to say they'd be late and started up to that newish, elegant and very expensive hotel.

Palliser and Grace had started out to find that security guard. The old Sam Goldwyn Studios were in county territory even if they were in the middle of Hollywood, on Santa Monica Boulevard. They didn't know if the studio was being used for anything these days; maybe some of the TV soaps got filmed there. At any rate there was a uniformed guard at the front entrance, and he looked at the badges in surprise.

''When does your shift change?'' Palliser asked.

''Six o'clock, the other three guards take over then, why do the cops want to know?''

''Is one of them about thirty, six feet, husky, with dark hair?''

''Well, I guess that could maybe be Eddy Lopez. What the hell do cops want with Eddy? He's a good guy.''

''We just want to talk to him,'' said Grace. ''He'll be on at six? We'll be back.''

The guard grinned. ''It won't do you any good, it's his night off. There's a substitute on for him.''

''Oh, hell,'' said Palliser.

The guard didn't know where Lopez lived, but all the guards came from the same security service and that office would have his address. Unfortunately, the office was closed on Saturday. They talked to the other two guards on duty and neither of them knew Lopez's address. There were two pages of Eduardo, Ed, and E.

Lopez's in just the Hollywood and Central phone books.

"Tomorrow," said Grace philosophically. "At least he'll be here on duty at six P.M."

"And at least we know who he is," said Palliser.

Saturday night could be busy for the Robbery-Homicide night watch. It started out with a brawl in a bar, with a man knifed: nothing complicated about it, but it added up to assault and would make some paperwork and take up some time. Then one of the squads called in a dead body, in a car parked on Virgil; Conway went to look at it and it was just a kid, about eighteen. It looked like an overdose. The damn-fool kids using the dope. There wasn't any I.D. on him but they got a make on the car from Sacramento and it was registered to a Juanita Cordova at an address in Hollywood. Conway went up to talk to her and brought her down to the morgue, and she identified the body as her son Carlos.

"He take all these terrible pills, *sí*," she said, sobbing. "I don't know why the kids got to take this terrible stuff."

That took up some more time, and then at ten o'clock they were called out to a heist at a pharmacy on Olympic. The pharmacist was a man about sixty, tall and thin, and he was more disgusted than scared. He said, "We keep this place open at night as a convenience to the public, for the Lord's sake, up to midnight for emergencies. And do they appreciate it, do we get much business after six o'clock? No damn way. Do you think I enjoy giving up my evenings at home to mind the store? Well, I damn well don't. The time was I thought of my profession as something like a doctor's, helping human suffering, but I guess I've changed my mind. Just last night, I'm just closing up the place when a fellow lands here swearing at me because the door is locked, he's got to get the prescription filled right away, save his wife's life, and it's just a damned tranquilizer. I own this place, and I'm going back to keeping civilized hours, close up at six." There had been two heisters, and he couldn't give a very good description of either of them: just a pair of young fellows, he said, with a gun. He didn't know anything about guns. They'd taken the cash, and a lot of the uppers

94

and downers from the pharmacy stock; that was as good as cash on the street.

The rest of the shift was quiet.

Verna Tyson had nearly decided not to go to work tonight. Last night she'd had a windfall, she'd run across a guy, a young guy on shore leave from the Navy, and made the deal with him, and when he'd had a few drinks he'd got all happy and talkative, and when he'd left her pad he'd slipped her two fifty-dollar bills. She'd picked up another one earlier, for the standard deal of thirty-five, so that was a good night's work.

She was twenty-nine. She didn't particularly enjoy the job, but it was a living and at least you didn't have to get up early in the morning. She didn't have much education; she'd grown up in various foster homes around Chicago, and been drafted into the job by a handsome pimp back there. But she'd soon enough found out what that was like, the money doled out grudgingly by the pimp, and she'd got away and come west and was doing all right by herself.

It was force of habit made her get dressed up and go out, about eight o'clock. She had dinner at one of her regular places, a bar and grill on Temple, and ran into a girl she knew, Nita Gomez, and they talked some. They talked about this crazy man killing the girls; there had been something about it in the newspapers but Verna didn't read too good. But all the girls had heard this and that about him. Nita said, "I even heard he cuts their heads off—*¡Jesús y María!* But the way I figure, he's crazy so he must look crazy, you know? You just got to be careful, not take up with nobody looks crazy."

"I guess you're right," said Verna. Neither of them was particularly intelligent, and it didn't occur to them that the other girls wouldn't havé made the deal with an obvious lunatic.

About ten o'clock a man came into the bar where Verna was still sitting nursing the last of a glass of cheap wine, and he looked around and then came over to her table. He said in a soft voice, "Can I buy you another drink?"

Verna sized him up and said, "Sure." He brought back a half bottle of the cheap wine and sat down at the table. He looked like a good prospect. He was very neat and clean, in a gray suit and white shirt and blue necktie; he looked as if he might work in an office somewhere, and he was carrying a kind of briefcase; he put that down beside his chair. Maybe he was about thirty-five, clean shaven, and he had a quiet soft voice.

He asked easily, "What's the going price, dear?"

Verna said, because he looked a lot higher-class than the ones she usually ran across, "Maybe fifty."

"That's okay," he said. So what with last night's take, she'd be some ahead of the game. She took a swallow of the thin sharp wine. And then all of a sudden she began to have a very funny feeling about this guy. She couldn't put a finger on it. He was sure a cut above the usual type of johns she ran into, he was quiet and mild and polite. Could be he was one of the kinky ones, but you had to put up with that. Just, all of a sudden, she didn't like him no way. She wasn't afraid of him, that was silly, but for some reason she didn't like him.

She said, "Thanks for the drink, but I just decided to take the night off. It's no deal."

He sat very quiet, watching her in the dim light of the bar. "Why?" he asked.

"No reason, I just decided. It's no deal. Get lost, mister."

He got up and went out of the place. Verna decided she really would take the night off. She could afford to.

Chapter 6

Looking for ammunition to use on Eddy Lopez when they picked him up, on Sunday morning Palliser and Grace went out to that duplex to talk to the Hesses again. Mrs. Hess said positively that she would say that nobody but that man had come to the other side of the duplex on Friday afternoon, and she'd seen him drive away about three o'clock. She said she'd recognize him if she ever saw him again. Back at the office, Palliser called the coroner's office and talked to one of the doctors about the corpse, and the doctor said, "I just finished the autopsy, we'll get a report to you sometime. Well, we can pin down the time of death for you pretty tight, by the digestive processes. She died between two-thirty and three-thirty, and probably nearer three, and she'd had sexual intercourse shortly before death."

"Thanks very much," said Palliser. He passed that on to Grace. "It looks open and shut, Jase. With the husband out of it, it's got to be this Lopez. They had an argument, and he didn't mean to kill her but he did."

"That's what it looks like," agreed Grace. "We'll be doing some overtime on this. Pick him up when he comes on the job at six."

They'd all heard about the new information on the werewolf, and did some talking about that incredible thing. Wanda Larsen was off on Sunday. Calhoun took Landers along to the arranged lineup at the jail. The witnesses to the heist showed up and without any hesitation identified Juan Diaz as the heister. It was always gratifying to catch up to one of them. They booked him formally and went back to the office, and Calhoun applied for the warrant. There were still two heists to work. Nothing had resulted so far from the sketch of the beautiful redhead or the photos of Carpenter, but it was early to expect anything. Mendoza came in; he was still feeling amused about those bank heisters. Hackett had passed that one on to the rest of them.

"They were surprised as hell to get dropped on—the damn fools still right here in town, living it up with their girls about twelve blocks from where they'd pulled the job, for God's sake, having a fling with the loot." It might have ruined Gerber's evening, but it was satisfying to have them stashed in jail. Those two would be going back to a federal pen after a simple hearing.

The pharmacist from last night's heist came in to make a statement, and Higgins talked to him, typed it up for him to sign. For the moment there wasn't much to do until they picked up Lopez. But with the heat going up, they could expect new business, and about eleven o'clock a new call went down to a dead body. Landers and Galeano went out to see what it was.

It was on the street, midway in a block of Sixth just down from Rampart, and there was a little crowd of about eight witnesses. On Sunday morning there wouldn't be the usual crowds in the street. There were two cars angled into the curb in a loading zone, an old Chevy and an older Ford, and the squad car was double-parked. The Traffic man was Dubois. He said to Landers, "There was a little accident and they all got mad about it, what I gather. The dead one's a Carlos Avila." The body was lying up against the curb, the body of a man about forty, a nondescript body dressed in ordinary clothes, brown pants and a white T-shirt. "The other two are Pedro Ortiz and Robert Shaver," said Dubois.

"So what happened?" asked Landers.

"Little accident," said Dubois. "I had to use a little persuasion to calm Ortiz down, he was going for Shaver with a knife, I understand from a couple of witnesses. They were just walking down the street and saw it happen, and seeing Ortiz is twice Shaver's size, they jumped in on the side of the underdog and pulled him off. Somebody else called us."

Ortiz was big and broad. Shaver was black, a thin young fellow leaning on the back of the Chevy.

"So what happened here?" asked Galeano.

Ortiz said roughly, "We was just on our way to see some friends, Carlos and me, we share a pad, and we was goin' to see Carlos' sister and her girl friend, we were goin' down to the beach. This black bastard, he starts to pass us, and he cut in too quick and nicks the front bumper and we get out and Carlos was cussing him and he took a swing at him and knocks him down, and by Jesus, Carlos don't get up and it looks as if he's dead, the damn black bastard—"

Shaver straightened up and protested, "That's just not so, I never touched him. It was my fault I hit their bumper, I kinda misjudged the distance, but there's no harm done and I stopped right away, and they both got out swearin' at me, callin' me names, and I tried to apologize—" He was a rather nice-looking young fellow in the twenties, neatly dressed. "That one, he come at me, he's goin' to hit me but then he just fell down against the curb."

"You knocked him down," said Ortiz furiously. "You hit him a good one and he fell down against the damned curb and busted his skull."

"All right, let's sort this out," said Landers sharply. "How many of you saw what actually happened?" Of the little crowd around four men said they'd seen it happen. Dubois called up another squad and they ferried them all back to the station to get statements, after the body had been taken away. The witnesses went reluctantly, annoyed at wasting their time. At the office Landers and Galeano roped Higgins in on the questioning, and they got a confused picture of what had happened. Ortiz insisted that Shaver had knocked Avila down, and Shaver insisted he hadn't touched him. "Look," he said, "would I have? He was a big guy and I'm not, and besides I was ready to apologize, it was my fault I hit them, I wasn't puttin' up any argument. He hadn't no call to get so damned mad. He was goin' to hit me and I was just trying to dodge him when all of a sudden he just fell down."

Three of the witnesses said Shaver had hit Avila and knocked him down, and the other one backed up Shaver, but that one was black and the other three were Latin. It took quite a while to get all the statements down. They got all the names and addresses and let them go, and Galeano said, "It'll be a question for the doctors. If Shaver did hit him there'll be a bruise showing and he probably died of a fractured skull."

In which case Shaver would be up for involuntary manslaughter, but that wasn't much of a charge. It was the tiresome sort of thing that took up a lot of time, caused a lot of trouble, all over nothing much at all. And now it was past lunchtime. Nobody else was in the office; probably they were all out to lunch.

Ordinarily they would have been out to lunch, and Hackett had just been thinking about it when Rita Putnam had relayed a call to him. "Sergeant Hackett," he said into the phone, and a male voice at the other end said cautiously, "Oh. What you a sergeant of?"

Surprised, Hackett said, "Police. Who is this?"

"Oh," said the voice uneasily. "Well, I don't know what this is all about, but he asked me to call you. You don't know me, my name's Crockett, I manage this apartment house on Grandview Avenue. And one of the tenants was just in here about five minutes ago and he said to call you and tell you Ollie's here. I don't know what it's about, that's just what he said. He said he couldn't be away more than three minutes, had to get right back, but I should call you and tell you that Ollie's here. He looked sort of funny, as if he was scared of something."

Hackett's mind made the connection and he asked, "Is his name Martin?"

"Yeah, that's right, William Martin. He's a good tenant, lived here for years, a quiet easygoing fellow. But he looked sort of funny. He just rang my bell and he handed me a little piece of paper and he says in a kind of whisper, please, Mr. Crockett, call this Sergeant Hackett and just tell him Ollie's here, do it right away please, he says, and he goes running back upstairs as if the devil

100

was after him. I don't know what in time it's all about."

Hackett said, "Thanks very much for calling, Mr. Crockett." That escaped con, Oliver Buckley. He told Higgins and Calhoun about it. "It sounds to me as if there's something a little funny going on there. Martin admitted he's afraid of Buckley. Is Buckley holding him hostage some way? But if he was, and Martin got away long enough to see the manager, why in hell did he go back to the apartment—why didn't he call us himself?"

"Well, whatever," said Higgins, "we can guess that one like Buckley won't be without a gun. I think we'd all better roll on this just to be on the safe side."

Hackett and Calhoun thought so too. They rode over to the apartment on Grandview Avenue in Higgins' Pontiac, and there they talked to the manager, Crockett, who was a paunchy black man in the forties. "You said you thought Martin looked scared?" asked Hackett.

"Well, he sure did. Like I say, he's always been a quiet tenant, I hardly ever see him coming and going, he's a cook at some hospital. He's always right on time with the rent. Last time I saw him was when he paid the rent on the first of the month. But he looked funny just now, when he came. I think he was scared about something. What's it all about?" Hackett told him and he went a curious gray color. "Oh, my God, oh, my sweet Jesus, an escaped convict right here, and he's probably got a gun—oh, my Lord—"

"Well, we don't intend to have a gunfight unless we have to," said Higgins, and told him what they wanted him to do. He began to shake his head violently.

"I don't want nothing to do with it, count me out—"

"Now look," said Hackett, "it's the best chance to pick him up without any trouble, Mr. Crockett."

He took some persuading but finally agreed. They climbed the stairs behind him and stood at one side of the door while he rang the bell. After a moment the door opened a little crack, and they could see there was a chain on it inside.

"What is it?" asked a shaky voice.

"Mr. Martin," said Crockett tremulously, "it's some men

from the gas company, there's a leak somewhere in the building and they'll have to look at all the pipes.''

"No, they can't come in," said Martin. "I'm not feeling so good, I'm sick.''

"Please, Mr. Martin, they say there might be an explosion, you'd better let them look.''

There was a moment of silence and then Martin said back into the room, "You see I got to let them in, Ollie. It's all right,'' and he took the chain off the door and opened the door wider. Crockett slid away down the hall. Hackett, Higgins, and Calhoun surged through the door in a body. Across the little living room a big black man was sitting in an armchair, and he took one lightning look at them and came up shooting. Hackett felt a slug just graze the shoulder of his suit jacket. They'd gone in with guns out, and they all fired at him, and he was knocked back against the chair, slid down it, and sprawled on the floor.

"Oh, my dear Lord," said Martin, and passed out in a dead faint in the doorway to the kitchen. The little Chihuahua started to yip madly and pawed at him.

"Well, he's the one started it," said Higgins.

"And now, for God's sake," said Calhoun, "there'll be all the red tape on it.''

They looked at Buckley, who was very dead, with all three slugs in him and bleeding all over the floor. His gun was a Smith & Wesson Army model .45.

Crockett peered fearfully in at the door. "Oh, my God," he said, "did Mr. Martin get killed too?''

Hackett went to look at Martin. "He's just passed out, he'll be okay." Martin moaned and tried to sit up, and they helped him onto the couch. The dog jumped into his lap and he clutched it tightly.

"Is Ollie dead?" he asked weakly.

"Yes, he is," said Higgins. "When did he show up here?''

Martin sat up straighter. "It was his own doing. I promised Mother I'd always do what I could for him, but I was always afraid of him. You never knew what he'd do. And I'd never been so

102

scared in my life—the last four days—he came here that night, Wednesday, Wednesday night it was—and he was hurt, he'd done a holdup somewhere after he got out of prison, and whoever he held up had taken a shot at him and hit him in the arm—he said he'd stay here till it got better, he made me bandage it—and he made me call the hospital and say I was sick, couldn't come in to work. He knew if I could I'd tell you he was here, I wouldn't protect him from the law—''

"He's been holding you hostage?" asked Hackett.

Martin nodded dumbly. "He locked me in the bedroom at night and slept out here so I couldn't use the phone or get away while he was asleep."

"But you got away," said Calhoun. "Why the hell did you go back to the apartment, Mr. Martin?"

The tears were running down Martin's black face. "I had to, I had to," he said. "Like I had to come right back when I went to the market to get liquor for him—he said if I didn't come back right away, if I told the cops or anybody he was here—he'd shoot Pancho!" He was hugging the little dog. "Pancho's all I've got, all the family I've got, and I knew Ollie meant what he said—he was a bad man and ought to be shut away in prison. I told him I'd got behind on the rent and I'd promised Mr. Crockett to pay up today, he'd come up here if I didn't—and Ollie said I shouldn't be away more 'n five minutes or he'd shoot Pancho—I had to hurry right back."

"So that was it," said Calhoun. "He's a nice little dog, Mr. Martin."

"I never thought I'd say such a thing," said Martin, "but I'm thankful Ollie's dead. I'm just thankful it's all over."

It wasn't, of course, all over for the police.

"All the damned red tape," said Higgins, annoyed. They called the morgue wagon from the apartment and then Hackett talked to the coroner's office and told the doctor there about it.

"We don't have to spell it out for you. When you go for the slugs, label them which is which. We have to know which one of us actually accounted for him." The letter of the law had to be kept, and when they knew that, there'd have to be a hearing before the court: short and sweet, the inevitable label of justifiable homicide, but that was how the law read. Higgins told Martin and Crockett that they'd want formal statements from them; tomorrow would do.

The body was carted off; they collected Buckley's gun and went back to headquarters.

"The stupid violent punks going from bad to worse," said Calhoun in the elevator.

"It makes you wonder about genes," said Hackett. "Martin's a nice honest little man, and they had the same mother, same sort of bringing up."

"Waste of time to try to figure it out," said Higgins.

They didn't stop at the floor for their own office, but rode up to the lab. There, Scarne and Horder listened to the story and Scarne said, "So hand over the pieces." They all surrendered the guns. Hackett and Calhoun both carried the Colt Python .357 Magnum, Higgins the S. & W. Combat .357 Magnum. Scarne slapped temporary labels on all of them and took them away to fire the test slugs into the sandbags, label the results, and ten minutes later they got the guns back. As they rode down in the elevator, Higgins automatically took a box of extra ammo out of his pocket and reloaded the gun. "I haven't got any on me," said Calhoun. "There's a box in my desk."

"I was just thinking the other night," said Higgins, "those damn-fool British police going around without sidearms. It isn't once in a blue moon you have to pull the gun, but it's there if you need it, and you usually need it in a hurry. If we were British cops, right now we'd likely all be dead."

This kind of thing brought that home, and when they got to their own office Calhoun found the box of extra ammo, handed Hackett two slugs, and reloaded the Python. Higgins was on the phone to the local FBI office. He said to somebody there, "You can stop worrying about your escaped con from Indiana. He's dead. We just had a little gunfight with him and it was three to one."

104

It was three o'clock and none of them had had any lunch. Mendoza had just left half an hour ago; it was supposed to be his day off and he'd just dropped in to see what was going on. They were about to go up to the canteen for a snack to tide them over when Rita beckoned Hackett as they passed the switchboard. She was a rather pretty dark girl and Calhoun had done some automatic flirting with her, but just now she was looking a little sick. She said, "They just had a call from a squad downstairs. A homicide— it's your lunatic again."

"Oh, Christ," said Higgins.

Calhoun said sardonically, "Just as well we haven't had lunch. To have to look at a thing like that again—"

And Hackett said as if he still didn't believe it, "Forty-two!"

When Mendoza came in the back door of the big Spanish hacienda in the hills above Burbank, he found Mairí MacTaggart in the kitchen with baby Luisa.

"You'd best be warned to stay clear of her for a bit," said Mairí.

"Why?" asked Mendoza. "What's up? I noticed her car was back—did the party get called off?"

"Och, I don't know when I've seen her in such a temper," said Mairí. "But her mother was a McCann after all, she'll calm down in a bitty."

Curious, Mendoza went down the hall. In the big living room all four cats were sitting bolt upright on the couch, and Cedric was sprawled on the hearthrug. The twins were standing in the door of the dining room, Terry in her new green bathing suit, Johnny in his new green trunks; they'd been crying but not recently. Alison, her flaming red hair on end and the unexpected new one showing more prominently now, was pacing up and down the room swearing aloud in a mixture of Spanish and English.

"*¿Qué tienes?* What's the matter?" asked Mendoza cautiously.

She swung around to him. "I've never been so insulted in my life—*¡Qué atrocidad!* My God, the nerve of that woman—*¡Qué* *cara más dura!* Ordering us off her property as if we were peasants or something—the gall of that woman—"

"What happened?" asked Mendoza.

She went back to pacing." *Nunca he sido tan insultada*—I 've never seen such impudence, and of all the stupid things—because they can't swim! Looking down her nose at us and saying how astonished she was that they can't swim, she'd never have dreamed of inviting us if she'd known that, her two were swimming by the time they were three, and it's the most important thing to teach them as soon as they're walking— *Maldito sea,* you'd have thought she'd just found out they're retarded or something— Swimming!" said Alison furiously. "And she really couldn't take the responsibility, I'd better just take them home—ordering us off the property like stray dogs—they were just wading in the shallow end, and seven adults to keep an eye on them! I've never been so insulted—"

Johnny said mournfully, "We were havin' a good time in the pool and then the lady got cross and told us to go home and Mama said a lot of bad words to her."

"Knowing your mother, I believe you," said Mendoza. "I hope the lady doesn't understand Spanish."

Struck forcibly by that, Alison stopped in her tracks. "There, if I hadn't been so mad I'd have thought of that. Looked down my nose and said really, you don't speak Spanish, I thought any reasonably intelligent person— Swimming!" One thing the school had done for the twins was to straighten out their language; having bilingual parents, they had been somewhat confused until they had to use English all the time. "You'd have thought we'd neglected sending them to school or hadn't fed them properly, just because they can't swim! Bundling us off home—"

Johnny said, "It was fun wading, but all the other kids were swimming, and it looked like fun, but the lady was awful mad at Mama."

"Not half as mad as I was at her!" said Alison. "What's so damned important about swimming?"

106

Suddenly Terry started to cry again. "We was havin' a real good time there at first—and then Carla's mother got cross—and Carla said I was dumb because I can't swim—and I thought she was my bestest friend—"

Mendoza picked her up and settled her in his lap. "Never mind, *niña*, you have to take people as they are, as you'll find out when you're older."

"That Carla!" said Alison. "If ever I met an obnoxious child—she's just like her mother, a bossy little twerp. So they can't swim, what's the big deal, they're bright in school and at least they've got a lot better manners than that Carla!"

"Now calm down, *chica*," said Mendoza. *"Tiene su pizca de gracias,* it has its funny side." He got out his handkerchief to wipe Terry's eyes. Alison finally stopped pacing, flung herself down in a chair, and lit a cigarette.

"It's not worth crying over, Terry," she said. "You'll make other friends, and nicer ones than Carla. I suppose it is funny in a way, but honestly, Luis, the way she acted, the things she said—as if they're complete idiots just because they can't swim—"

Johnny said wistfully, "It looked like fun."

"The pool was so pretty," said Terry, sniffling.

"Now cheer up," said Mendoza briskly. "Suppose you change your clothes and go and find Ken and have a ride on the ponies." At their advent the ponies, Star and Diamond, had been a great success, but now the twins looked unenthusiastic.

"Maybe Mairí can find some cookies and milk for you," said Alison.

"That's right," said Mendoza. "Just try to forget about it, all of you. It's all over now." And those, of course, would turn out to be famous last words.

It was a carbon copy of all the others, as they had known it would be. This was an even shabbier place than Nadine Foster's, what used to be called an efficiency apartment, one small room with a daybed, a couple of chairs, a slit of a kitchenette off that, a tiny closet, a tiny bathroom. Higgins and Calhoun had come out on it, and they didn't look at it any longer than they had to. The head had been left on top of the chest of drawers, and the indecently pink intestines were draped over the chairs. Various organs had been cut out of the body and left beside it on the daybed.

The body had been found by the manageress of the apartment, Mrs. Schultz. It had belonged to an Agnes Metzger, not that the name was important. Both Higgins and Calhoun were simply thinking of it as number forty-two.

Mrs. Schultz was a little thin woman with a sharp nose, and she was still looking sick when they talked to her in her own apartment downstairs. They'd left the patrolman on the scene waiting for the lab men.

"I knew she was a prostitute," said Mrs. Schultz, "and I never thought I'd come to share a roof with a woman like that, but needs must when the devil drives like they say. My husband died ten years ago, he was only forty-six, and I can't get the Social Security yet, and I'd never worked while he was alive, I'd got no experience to get a job. I was lucky to get a job at all, I work at a cafeteria up on Grand, and I was lucky to get the job managing this place, I get the rent free. I knew what she was, but there were times I felt sorry for the woman at that. She wasn't young, I'd guess she was in her fifties anyway, and so I don't suppose she'd of found it easy—not that I know anything about that—but you know what I mean. She looked older than she probably was, she'd used so much makeup and never washed it off real good, and she used to get drunk when she had any money, I knew that, I'd seen her that way. And she was a month behind on the rent, and sorry or not I couldn't let it go on that way, I'm responsible to the people own this place. I'd spoken to her about it twice this week, and she said she'd try to get it somehow."

"Do you know where she went to pick up customers?" asked Higgins.

"I wouldn't know anything about that," she said primly. "She usually went out around nine o'clock at night, dressed up in what I suppose she thought were her best clothes—since it turned so warm, a cheap old nylon dress, bright red, and high-heeled shoes

108

all run over at the heels.''

"Did you ever see her come back with a man?" asked Calhoun.

She flushed. "Just once or twice. No, I didn't see her go or come last night. I went up about half an hour ago to ask her again about the rent, and she didn't answer—and the door was unlocked—and—" She pressed a handkerchief to her mouth— "Oh, my God, to see all that—all the blood—"

In the hall, Calhoun said, "The nearest bars are up on Temple or Alvarado. I don't suppose she'd have wanted to walk far in those high heels. Say it in spades, the werewolf isn't particular. Just anything female that's available. This one was another poor old lush on the way down."

Higgins said, "And we have to go through the motions, and I can hear the lab men swearing now. Another butcher shop to deal with, and they'll get just what they got on the others and no more."

The lab men arrived presently, Scarne and Horder, and did the expectable cussing. When they'd taken photographs they called the morgue wagon and had the body, or the various parts of it, hauled away for the doctors to deal with, so at least they wouldn't have to look at it while they went over the place. Just all the blood. It was after five, and Higgins and Calhoun went back to the office briefly and then called it a day. One of them would write the report tomorrow.

At five minutes of six, Palliser and Grace were waiting at the front gate of the Goldwyn Studios, when the day security guards were due to go off duty. Roberta and Virginia had been told that they wouldn't be seeing much of their husbands this evening. The three new guards arrived in their respective cars and parked in an open space off to one side of the gate. Eddy Lopez was easy to spot, the biggest of the three. He was a good-looking man with rather bushy dark hair and an olive complexion, broad-shouldered and competent-looking in his blue uniform. They both showed him the badges, and he said in surprise, "What do the cops want with me?"

"It's about Gladys Tucker," said Grace. "Do you know she's dead, Lopez?"

His naked astonishment might have been good acting. "Gladys? Dead? What the hell do you mean? I just saw her on Friday and she was fine then."

"She was murdered, Lopez," said Palliser. "Somebody strangled her, and we think you might know something about it."

He said stupidly, "Strangled—oh, my God—that's awful— Me? Me know something about it? You've got to be kidding. She was just fine when I left her on Friday."

"Well, we'll do some talking about it," said Palliser. "Let's go back to the station and talk about it."

"Listen, I can't just walk off the job like that, there are only three of us and we spell each other—"

"I'm afraid you'll have to," said Grace. "Come on, let's go."

None of them said a word on the way downtown, but when they took him up to the office, his expression had hardened and he looked wary. Schenke and Conway were playing gin on Higgins' desk. Palliser led Lopez down to one of the interrogation rooms, and he and Grace faced him across the little plastic table.

"We'll spell it out for you, Lopez," said Palliser evenly. "The Tucker girl had a lot of boyfriends and you were one of them. Every so often you'd meet her somewhere, pay for her lunch, and take her home to make out a little. You met her on Friday," and he named the place. "We've got witnesses who saw you leave together about one o'clock. We've got a witness who saw you both go into her place, and saw you leave at three o'clock. And the doctors tell us that was just about the time she was killed. Now what have you got to say about that?"

Lopez looked startled. He said, "There? Right there? But my God, it's crazy! All I can say is, you're just crazy if you think I did it. Why in hell should I want to hurt Gladys?"

"That's what we'd like to know," said Grace.

"It's just crazy." Lopez got out a cigarette and lit it, and his hands were trembling a little. "Look, I'll level with you guys, she was a good kid but I wasn't involved with her, if you know what I

110

mean. She was just an easy lay. Look, I don't know how much you know about her, but that one was a real nympho, she couldn't get enough of it. Yeah, I know she was married. She told me once she'd only married the guy for a meal ticket, so she didn't have to work. That didn't seem to worry her, and it was no skin off my nose. I know for a fact she had a lot of other guys on the string, she was making out with them too. All I can tell you, about Friday, she called me around ten A.M. when she knew I'd be up. We're on all night at the studio, but we spell each other like I say, doing rounds, and we've got a lounge with cots, I usually get three, four hours' sleep on the job, we all do. Spelling each other. Anyway, Gladys called me and said what about it, so I said I'd meet her. We had lunch at that place and went back to her pad just like you said. And I did leave about three. My God, she was a hot one, she wanted me to stay longer but I had things to do. I live alone and I have to do all my own marketing, and then I like to have early dinner and shower and change before going on the job, see. I left her about three, and she was just fine, kind of mad at me because I wouldn't stay on. She was lying on the bed stark naked and she waved me goodbye. All I can figure, right afterwards somebody else came in and killed her. Maybe her husband.''

"He's got an alibi," said Palliser. "And the witness next door says that nobody but you was there that afternoon, and she can identify you. That puts you right on the spot when she was killed, Lopez.''

He stared at them in growing dismay. "But it wasn't me—I swear to God it wasn't! I didn't have any reason to kill Gladys! She was just a girl, just an easy lay.''

"Maybe you had an argument over something," suggested Grace.

He shook his head violently. "No, I didn't. I didn't have any reason to argue with her, why should I? I wasn't involved with her, I tell you, I didn't feel much about her one way or the other, she was just an easy lay. When I left her she was just fine.''

They went on prodding at him for quite some time, and he just went on saying that over and over, and they came to a dead end.

Finally they called up a squad to take him back to Hollywood, and talked it over with Schenke and Conway. Piggott was out on a call.

"But it's got to be him," said Schenke, shuffling the pack for a new deal. "He was on the spot at the right time and nobody else was."

"He's a very tough customer," said Grace. "My guess is that something flared up between them—he says she wanted him to stay longer—it could be that she said something about his not having enough steam to prolong the session and he lost his temper. It's an easy way to kill somebody without intending to."

"That's very possible," said Palliser. "But it's all circumstantial evidence, Jase. I don't know if the D.A.'d go for any charge. If they do, it'd be voluntary manslaughter, not much of a charge. We'll ask the boss what he thinks about it."

The day men had left about nine-thirty. Piggott came back and told the others about the heist, and it wouldn't give anybody any work. It had been at a fast food place, and all the two men on duty could say was that the heister had been young and not very big; they wouldn't know him again. Apparently they were both so scared of the gun they hardly took their eyes off it. There might have been sixty or seventy bucks in the register.

They sat around awhile and Piggott typed a report on that. At eleven-thirty a new call went down, an assault. Conway took it. The address was Crandall Street, and it was a modest old single house. The patrolman waiting for him was Gibson. He was looking worried.

"I called the ambulance before I called you, where the hell is it? She doesn't look too good, I think she's been stabbed."

"So, do you know anything about what happened here?"

"Yeah, she's one hell of a spunky old lady. Her name's Mabel Ryerson, she lives here alone. She's the one called in. She's bleeding pretty bad but she managed to call in and she was still conscious when I got here, she'd even opened the front door for me. She told me she'd gone to bed but she couldn't get to sleep and she thought she'd get up and watch TV. She's deaf and she'd taken off

112

her hearing aid. When she got up and put it on and switched on a light, she found two burglars ransacking the place. They beat her up and stabbed her. I wish that damned ambulance would come. When she came to, they were gone, and she managed to dial and I got shot out here.''

''The damned punks,'' said Conway. They went into the house. The old lady was lying on the couch in the living room. Her eyes were closed and her pulse was shallow; she was just a little old white-haired woman. She had on a nightgown and an old chenille bathrobe, and there was a good deal of blood showing. The room was a shambles; the burglars always left the mess.

But she was still conscious. She opened her eyes and looked up at them. ''You take it easy, ma'am,'' said Gibson. ''The ambulance will be here in a minute.''

She said in a faint but clear voice, ''They called each other Ron and Joe. It was lucky I had on my hearing aid or I wouldn't have heard that. They were both black.''

The ambulance came then and took her off, and there wasn't much to do on this tonight but call the lab, and those men would be annoyed; it was nearly the end of their shift, they couldn't do much on it tonight. If the old lady didn't die, sometime they'd get her to tell them what was missing, and get a better description of the burglars. Gibson called the lab from the squad, and Duke came out in a van, cussing. ''You should find some keys somewhere,'' said Conway. ''Just lock up the place when you leave.''

''Now I'll tell you, John,'' said Mendoza on Monday morning, ''I don't think the hell of a lot of it. It would add up to voluntary manslaughter, and I'll agree with both of you it has to be Lopez on Gladys Tucker. He's placed on the spot at the right time and nobody else is. But that's circumstantial and I don't think the D.A.'s office would waste time on it. We can ask, of course. I'll see what they say.''

He was deflected from that immediately by Higgins and Calhoun giving him the details about Agnes Metzger, number forty-two; but there was nothing in that, and the lab would be telling them just what they'd told them before.

Then he got on the phone to Duffy at the D.A.'s office, at eleven o'clock, and spent nearly an hour kicking the Tucker thing around with him. Duffy took down all the relevant facts and said they'd talk it over and decide if there was enough for a charge. He'd get back to Mendoza sometime.

There was nothing in from the card rooms, or the men on the Seventy-seventh Street beat, on those photos of Jerome Carpenter. Nobody on their beat, apparently, had spotted the gorgeous redhead with the big gun.

And there wasn't any point in hashing over what they knew about their werewolf. Mendoza looked over Higgins' report on Agnes Metzger and filed it away.

He had just started out for lunch with Hackett and Higgins, and they were talking about Carpenter. "It was just damn bad luck," said Higgins angrily, "that Gunther didn't take down the plate number. If we'd had that, we'd have caught up to the bastard by now—"

And Mendoza stopped dead, the Homburg in his hand, and said, "*¡Diez millones de demonios!* I'm going senile in my old age—but all of the rest of you should have thought of it, for God's sake—"

"What?" asked Hackett.

"*Por Dios*—the stake from getting hot at poker—what he told the Garcias— *Vaya por Dios,* he'd been over at Vegas—if he'd been there long, there might be a car registered to him in Nevada—and ask about both names just in case—" Mendoza fled back to his office, told Farrell to get him Carson City. In five minutes the DMV there wired them a make on a car registered to Andy Dickinson, a seven-year-old Buick. And five minutes later they had an A.P.B. out on it.

Chapter 7

They were all just drifting back from lunch when a brief report came in from the lab about the gunfight yesterday. It had been the slug from Calhoun's gun that had killed Buckley. He'd got him in the heart. Higgins had hit his left shoulder and Hackett his midchest. Calhoun let out some heartfelt cusswords. "So I have to waste a day in court on the damned red tape!"

And there was the new one to think about, the common assault by the burglars. Hackett called the hospital to see how the old woman was doing, and a doctor told him that they didn't know yet whether she'd make it, she'd lost a good deal of blood and been in shock. So that might turn into a homicide.

Mendoza was still feeling triumphant over his brainwave about the Nevada license plate. "By God, this has got to turn up Carpenter," he said. Galeano managed to simmer him down long enough to tell him the gist of that rigmarole yesterday, the little street accident and the dead man, Carlos Avila. "It's not much of a thing, but these eyewitness accounts—"

"And you know how much they're worth as a rule," said Mendoza cynically. "It'll depend on what the doctors say. It's not much of a thing, if Shaver did knock him down and it's a fractured skull, we'll have him up for involuntary manslaughter, that's all."

"Well, that's what Tom and I both thought," said Galeano. "I don't suppose we'll get the autopsy report until tomorrow or next day."

Mendoza said, "And preserve our souls in patience on Carpenter." He was restless, roaming around the office, smoking too much. The witnesses to the heist last night came in to make statements, and Landers talked to them. Mendoza reread Conway's report on that assault last night and asked Hackett, "Has anybody done any follow-up on this? If the woman's got any relatives they ought to be informed."

"I've got no idea," said Hackett. He called the lab and asked Marx about it. "Well, Duke started on it but he hadn't finished dusting the place, I think Scarne's over there now. I don't know if anybody came across an address book."

Hackett got up with a sigh. This was part of the job too. He found the address on Crandall Street, and there was just one neighbor home at the house next door, a middle-aged woman named Martinez who said concernedly, "Oh, that's a terrible shame, Mrs. Ryerson bein' hurt like that, I'm sorry. I don't know her too good but I think she's got a daughter back east somewhere, not right around here anyway."

Scarne was still in the house, the mobile lab van parked in front. Hackett asked him if he'd come across an address book and he said, "Beside the phone in the hall, it's been printed." Hackett looked through it and the only out-of-state address was for a June Shelley, in Rockford, Illinois. He called the number and talked to her. She was the daughter, and she was upset but level-headed.

"Of course we'll come right out," she said. "We didn't like her living alone, but she's so independent—we'll come as soon as we can get a plane."

Hackett went back to the office and relayed that to Mendoza. "And on number forty-two, I suppose we ought to ask around the local bars, if anybody noticed her pick up the john that night."

"Nobody will have," said Mendoza. "You know that, Art. And the type she was, he may have picked her up on the street. The only way we're going to catch up to the werewolf is if

116

Nemesis takes after him, or he begins to slip up.''

"You've always been superstitious,'' said Hackett.

"And on second thought,'' said Mendoza, "maybe we can find a shortcut on that assault.'' He was rereading Conway's report. "I think I'll go talk to somebody down in Burglary.''

Two floors down in that office he was eventually handed over to a Lieutenant Navarro, a big dark fellow with shrewd eyes, who asked, "What can we do for Robbery-Homicide?'' Mendoza handed over the report.

"I know they're common names—Ron and Joe—and you're just as busy as we are with quite a turnover, but I just thought I'd ask if it rings a bell.''

"Well, if you ask me, I'd say we're busier,'' said Navarro. "The burglary rate is climbing sky high all over. But just as it happens, I think we can do you some good here. Ron and Joe.'' He stroked his thick jaw reflectively. "The burglars are usually loners. They're common names all right, but this could ring a bell kind of loud and clear. Ron Scott and Joe Cooper. They've run together for quite awhile, they're fairly stupid lowlifes, they've both served time in for the burglaries. We picked them up last about a year ago, they were just out of the joint then. Reason I made the connection right off, God knows they're the typical punks and we see all too many like them, but Scott kind of interests me on account of that girl.''

"What girl?'' asked Mendoza.

Navarro chuckled. "Of course, what mere male can understand women, but it's a damned funny thing. Her name's Geraldine Brock, and she's a fairly nice girl, Mendoza. She's got no record, she works honest jobs. She's Scott's girl friend. She knows all about him, he's been in trouble with us on one count or another since he was about fourteen—possession, assault, break-ins, and you'd think a girl like that wouldn't want anything to do with him. But she gives him money when he's broke, she'd do anything for him, it doesn't matter what he's been up to. She's made bail for him a few times.''

117

"The vagaries of females," said Mendoza. "Would you have a current address for this pair?"

"You can ask R. and I.," said Navarro. "But I seem to remember the girl was working at a Thrifty drugstore on Wilshire last year."

"So thanks very much for the cooperation," said Mendoza. He went back to his own office and passed that on to Hackett.

Hackett said, "Well, a place to look. If the old lady pulls out of it she may be able to identify them." It was four-thirty; he got up resignedly. "I may as well have a look for the girl, she'll probably know where Scott is anyway."

There was a Thrifty drugstore a little out of their beat on Wilshire; he drove up there and went in to ask. The manager told him that Geraldine Brock worked there, but it was her day off. He could give Hackett her address, on Baxter Drive in the Silver Lake area. It was then after five but Hackett went up there, found it was an eight-unit apartment. Geraldine Brock wasn't home, and the only other tenant home didn't know her or where she might be. Hackett didn't bother to go back to the office, but started toward home. He was glad to get there, to the sprawling house on the dead-end street in Altadena. The children, Mark and Sheila, were chasing around the backyard with the monstrous mongrel, Laddie, and in the kitchen Angel said, "You're a little early. Rough day?"

He kissed her and said, "Just more of the usual." But thank God it had cooled off some.

Calhoun and Grace were both off on Tuesday. The night watch hadn't left them anything new. The hospital was now saying that Mrs. Ryerson was stabilized and doing better, but they couldn't question her until tomorrow. "She's probably told us all she could anyway," said Landers; they had all heard what she'd had to say about the burglars. "If she can identify this pair it won't matter whether we can tie up any of the loot to them. We'd better get hold of this girl, she'll know where Scott is living." He went out on that with Galeano.

118

At that Thrifty out on Wilshire they asked for the Brock girl. She was at the tobacco counter, a slim black girl about twenty-five with a round pretty face and a nice figure. She looked at Landers' badge, listened to the questions, and asked in obvious distress, "Ron's in trouble again? He's always getting in trouble, I wish he wouldn't, it's just that he's kind of weak, that's all. But I kind of suspected something was wrong, he'd been up to something, when he came to see me yesterday."

"Is that so?" said Galeano. "Did he say anything about doing a burglary or whatever?"

"Oh, no, he wouldn't, he knows I don't like him doing things against the law. But"—and she looked at them with mournful dark eyes—"I suspected something kind of unusual had happened, because he'd took a bath. He don't hardly ever take a bath, maybe a couple of times a year, but he'd took one, he was all clean and had on clean clothes."

Landers and Galeano started to laugh and she said, "I don't see what's so funny."

Galeano managed to control himself. "Do you know where he's living?"

"Sure, he and Joe Cooper share a pad together, just a room, it's a rooming house on Magnolia."

On the way back to the car Landers said, "My God, Nick, we should be able to trace him by the smell."

"What gets into women?" said Galeano. "She's a nice-looking honest girl, why she should take up with one like that—it does make you wonder."

But at the rooming house on Magnolia neither Scott nor Cooper was at home, and nobody knew where they might be.

There had been a heist on the street last night, a middle-aged couple held up in the parking lot of a restaurant on Beverly, and they came in in early afternoon to make a statement. Wanda talked to them and typed it up. They had just signed it and left when she had a call from Juvenile.

It was Ruth Gordon; they'd been at the Academy together. Ruth was a fairly tough and experienced juvenile officer, married to a sergeant in Hollenbeck Division, but she was sounding shaken now. "We've got some business for you," she said. "It's one hell of a thing, Wanda. I suppose you'll want to turn the lab loose on it. We've just brought all the kids in, there are twelve of them all under fifteen, we left the squad-car man to preserve the scene for you."

"So what's the story?" asked Wanda.

"One of the neighbors called in a complaint about the noise, some kind of wild party going on, and when the patrolman got there he didn't like the look of it and called us. There were all these kids, most of them high on something, no adults around, the rock music going full blast. Myra and I went out on it with Sergeant Peck, and it's a mess, Wanda—you'd better go look at it. There's a body in the garage."

"For heaven's sake," said Wanda. "All right, we'll get back to you."

Palliser was the only one in at the moment, and they went out to see what this was. The house was a small stucco place on a narrow lot, and the patrolman standing guard over it was Armstrong. He said, "You'll probably want to talk to their neighbors both sides, it's a Mrs. Estrada and a Mrs. Fischer."

"Let's see the body first," said Palliser.

"It's in the garage." Armstrong led the way up the narrow drive paved with cracked cement. It was a single detached garage, and about all it contained was an old Ford sedan. In the back seat was the body of a woman lying on its back. She looked as if she was in the late thirties, dark-haired and slender. She was wearing a nightgown and a shabby nylon bathrobe, and there was a knife sticking out of her chest. Palliser told Armstrong to call the lab, and he and Wanda went to talk with the neighbors.

The neighbors were together at Mrs. Estrada's house. They were both middle-aged. "It was just too much," said Mrs. Fischer. "That awful rock music, you could hear it half a block away, turned up so loud, and when it went on all last night I won-

120

dered, because Mrs. Jenkins wouldn't have put up with it. I rang the doorbell yesterday and that girl answered, her name's Cynthia, she's about fourteen, she's Mrs. Jenkins' daughter, they lived there together. Mrs. Jenkins, she works at some hotel as a maid, she's divorced. And the girl said her mother wasn't home—she was rude as could be—''

"And today," said Mrs. Estrada with extravagant gestures, "when the music goes on, we think why not the kids in school? It's school day—we think something wrong—''

"Which there was," said Wanda.

Reluctantly the women followed them back, and identified the body as Rose Jenkins. "But that girl!" said Mrs. Estrada. "Her own mama!''

The lab van came with Marx and Horder in it and they looked over the house. It was in a mess. There were LP records scattered all around, the remains of pizzas and hamburgers. On the coffee table in the living room was a generous supply of reefers, and on the fake mantle, bottles of the uppers and downers. There were full and empty liquor bottles, gin and vodka. "Kids!" said Palliser. "I tell you, Wanda, it makes you feel a little scared of being a parent.''

They left the lab men going over the place, taking the photographs of the body, and went back to Parker Center and up to the Juvenile bureau. Ruth Gordon and Myra Taylor were waiting for them. "What a thing," said Ruth. She was pretty and blond, Myra dark and older. "You can't talk to any of the kids yet, all of them were high on this or that, the liquor or dope, so it isn't admissible evidence that the girl said, 'Tommy stuck a knife in mother.' She was giggling about it.''

"Dear Lord," said Wanda. "You sent them all over to Emergency.''

"What else?" said Myra. "Twelve of them. Around thirteen or fourteen. The neighbors said the rock music had been going on since Sunday night, so probably that's how long the woman had been dead. And they knew the Jenkins woman had had trouble with the girl over her getting into drugs.''

"Doing what comes naturally," said Palliser. "We don't have to talk to them, do we? We can read it. Maybe a couple of the girl's friends there, including Tommy, and the woman telling them to cut down the noise, or finding them smoking the joints, and she got the knife to stop her arguing at them."

"And they've been having a ball ever since," said Wanda. "When they're sobered up, we'll have to talk to them, but they're all minors." They knew how that would go. Sort out Tommy, who'd done the actual killing, and he'd be held in custody until he was of age, or possibly just get probation. The others—the Juvenile officers would have a hassle with the parents. It didn't seem as if any of them could be very responsible parents, not knowing or caring where their kids were, and in the end some of the kids might end up in the foster homes. "Did the Jenkins woman have any relatives?" asked Wanda.

"The neighbors don't know. The divorced husband had visitation rights but he wasn't around much."

"What a mess," said Wanda. "Well, between us we'll have to sort it out."

"The kids," said Palliser again. "I'm really not old enough to start saying what's the next generation coming to. Just let us know when we can talk to them."

"We'll be in touch on it," said Myra.

Ron Scott and Joe Cooper still hadn't come home to the rooming house. So far none of the squads anywhere in the county had spotted that Nevada plate.

The autopsy report on Gladys Tucker came in, but that just told them what they already knew. They'd have to wait for the autopsy report on Carlos Avila to know whether there'd be a charge on that or not.

Mendoza left the office a little early, and when he got home to the big Spanish house, the twins were out riding their ponies in the ring beside the corral, under the supervision of Ken Kearney. In the deserted kitchen he poured himself a couple of fingers of rye, and El Señor arrived at a dead run, demanding his share. Mendoza

122

went down the hall and found Alison slumped in her armchair doing nothing.

"*¿Qué tal, querida?*"

"My heavens above," said Alison, "I could cheerfully strangle that Coatesworth woman! What she started—"

The twins, having seen him drive in, came erupting down the hall. "Daddy, we got an idea!" They came tugging at him from both sides. "Daddy," said Johnny imperiously. "You got enough money, Ken says—"

"Daddy"—and Terry climbed into his lap—"we got an idea, we want to build a swimming pool! The pool there was so pretty, and if we had one, there couldn't nobody tell us we couldn't be in it—"

"You see," said Alison bitterly.

"*Qué diablos,*" said Mendoza. "You hold it right there, both of you! No. I refuse to clutter up the place with one of those monstrosities."

"But it was so pretty!" said Terry. "All blue and shiny and pretty blue tiles—"

"And we could practice and learn how to swim," said Johnny. "And then we could tell people to go home, if it was our own pool—"

"*Dios me libre,*" said Mendoza. "No! We may indulge you in some ways—and when I think what those ponies cost—but I put my foot down on this."

"Please!" said Terry, and her big brown eyes were melting, threatening tears. "Please, Daddy."

Mendoza swallowed rye and said firmly, "No."

"You saying it was all over," said Alison. "I could strangle the woman. Once they get an idea in their heads—"

"They can keep this idea in their heads for the next year," said Mendoza. "No swimming pool. You can just forget about it, *niños,* and if either of you starts to cry I'll spank you."

"I'll bet you wouldn't really," said Johnny.

* * *

The night watch left them two new heists to work. Nothing had come in overnight on that A.P.B. It was Hackett's day off. About eleven o'clock, Duffy at the D.A.'s office called Mendoza. "About this Tucker homicide," he said, "we're not going to move on it, Mendoza. It was Lopez did it, of course, but the evidence is all circumstantial and all it would add up to is voluntary manslaughter. He's got no record, never been in any trouble, and it's unlikely he'd serve any time for it. It'd be a waste of the court's time. Just file the paperwork away and forget it."

"That's what I thought you'd say," said Mendoza. He went out to the communal office to pass that on. Wanda was talking to a witness. Higgins and Calhoun had just come back from somewhere. "The D.A.'s not interested in charging Lopez," said Mendoza.

Higgins said, "Hell. And not that I suppose the woman was much loss to the world, but just naturally I don't like to see anybody get away with homicide."

Calhoun was sitting smoking with his eyes shut. "Maybe nobody will," he said lazily. "Lopez didn't kill her, you know. The husband killed her."

"Now, Pat," said Higgins patiently, "he's got an alibi. I checked it myself."

Calhoun opened his eyes and grinned at him. "I tell you," he said, "you're a lot farther away from your school days than I am. I've had a little idea about this all along. I don't think Tucker's got any alibi at all. If we chase over to that school maybe we can prove it."

"I don't get you," said Higgins.

"Let's go and see," said Calhoun. Mendoza was curious enough to tag along.

The elementary school on Union Street, like all other public schools, had a great bare expanse of playground on three sides of it. There was a parking lot for the teachers and other personnel at one side, and besides the two-story main building, there were framed bungalows to take the overflow of students, and one wing built on to the main building. They went in the front entrance. The

124

corridor ahead of them was deserted. The registrar's office and principal's office were just inside to the left, both doors shut. There was a low hum behind the closed doors of the classrooms on either side, but nobody was in sight. Calhoun led them up to the end of the corridor, looking into a door labeled *Teachers' Lounge*, another labeled *Boys' Restroom*, without encountering any of the maintenance crew. It wasn't until they had climbed to the second floor that they found Pete Lacey pushing an oversized mop along the hall floor. He straightened, recognizing Higgins.

"You're that cop. Have you found out about Sam's wife yet? He hasn't come back to work, I guess he's all broken up."

Calhoun said, "We'd just like to ask you a couple of more questions. How do you lay out the work here? It's a pretty big building."

Lacey leaned on the mop handle. "It sure is, and I often thought it'd be a better idea to have us come on at night when the kids aren't here to get in our way. But they're always making a mess, leave things in the hall, papers and candy wrappers, and the trash bins are always getting full. How do we arrange different jobs, you mean? Well, I generally check the second floor mornings and afternoons, and Denny does the ground floor and Sam's in the other wing. You know, we have to clean up the restrooms half a dozen times a day, the kids are little pigs. And keep the halls clean and all. In the winter there's the furnace in the basement to keep an eye on, and right now the air-conditioning system."

"Where do you have lunch?" asked Calhoun. There was dawning comprehension in Higgins' eyes.

"We eat in the cafeteria, that's in the other wing. After the kids are through, that's at one o'clock. The kitchen staff all leave by one-thirty, they're all part-time, you know. Then Denny and me go back to the main building and Sam cleans up in the cafeteria and kitchen."

"That would be some time after one-thirty?"

"That's right."

"So," said Higgins suddenly, "how long would it be before either of you saw Tucker again? To see and talk to?"

Lacey looked puzzled. "Why, he'd be busy over there for a couple of hours, usually. Depending on how much of a mess the kids left."

"Do you remember, last Friday afternoon," asked Calhoun, "after you and Rios went back to the main building, when was the next time you saw Tucker?"

Lacey ruminated. "Why, next time I saw him was when we all came out to the parking lot together about five of four. Why? He was here whether I saw him or not."

"And where would Rios be about now?"

"Probably doing one of the restrooms downstairs." He stared after them curiously.

They found Rios just coming out of a girls' restroom on the ground floor. He said, "Friday?" and thought. "We all had lunch at the cafeteria, I guess we finished about one-thirty, and Pete and me went back to the main building. Sam, he got the cleaning stuff, mop and broom and so on, and started cleaning up the cafeteria."

"When did you see him again?"

"Why, it'd be when we all left together about four. He was already in the parking lot when Pete and me come out."

"Thanks very much," said Calhoun. They started back down the hall. "Hey presto, the quickness of the hand deceives the eye. Tucker hasn't any more alibi than the man in the moon."

Mendoza was laughing. "Aren't you so right, we're too far removed from our school days to have thought of that, Pat—the size of a place like this, and the maintenance crew wandering around."

"He must have had some suspicion what kind she was," said Calhoun. "He was checking up on her. And if he walked in on her and found her naked in bed—just after Lopez had left—"

"Yes, I think you've got something," said Higgins.

"He'll keep," said Mendoza. "Let's have lunch before we tackle him."

They got to the shabby old duplex at two o'clock, and as they came up the narrow front walk, Calhoun said, "She isn't a magician, you know. Mrs. Hess next door. She may be a nosy neighbor, but she can't be in two places at once. All she told us was, nobody but Lopez came or went by the front way."

Mendoza was laughing again. "Don't rub our noses in it, Pat. We see it, we see it." He pushed the doorbell. After a long moment the door opened and Tucker looked at them. He looked thinner, and somehow shrunken. "We've got a few more questions for you," said Higgins.

He stood back silently, and they went in to the small square living room with its sparse shabby furniture. Tucker sat down on the couch and stared at the floor. "What is it?" he asked without much interest.

"You weren't at work all day Friday, were you?" asked Higgins. "Lacey and Rios never saw you at all from about one-forty until you all met in the parking lot at four o'clock. You came home, didn't you? You suspected your wife was cheating on you, and you slipped away from work and drove home to check up on her. Didn't you?"

Tucker didn't look up. He was silent for a long minute, and then he said in a dull voice, "I was afraid you'd find out about it. Yes, I did. She was driving me crazy, I couldn't stand it no longer. She never even tried to cover it up—she bragged about it, how many fellows she had. I'd thought she was a nice girl, I was in love with her when we got married. And then—and then I found out about her. And I—she made me too ashamed—to do anything about it. How did it make me look, to my family and everybody, have it come out in the open, how she'd fooled me? I'd of looked like a goddamned fool. And I still—I guess—sort of loved her—She was the prettiest girl ever had any time for me. But it was driving me crazy. All the time I was at work I'd be thinking about her bringing other fellows home—she didn't care how it made me feel, and sometimes when I came home she'd laugh at me, tell me the one with her today was a hundred percent better than me— And it got so I couldn't stand it." He was still looking at the floor, shoulders hunched.

Calhoun asked, "When did you get here?"

He didn't answer directly. "I was working in the cafeteria, and it was going round and round in my head, it was just too much. I

127

knew she had some man there right then, and I just left everything and got my car and drove home. There was a car in front of the house. I went round the block and parked and came across the vacant lot behind here. She never kept the doors locked. I came in the back quiet—and I—and—and I heard him leave.''

"Three o'clock," said Higgins softly.

"It'd be about then. I heard him say goodbye to her and go out the front door. And when I went into the bedroom, she was lying there naked, she was surprised to see me, she said what are you doing here—and I—just couldn't stand to think of it, what she'd been doing, what she'd done to me—and I just took hold of her—'' He was silent again and then finished painfully. "And when I saw she was dead—I just thought, go back to work—and maybe nobody'd ever think I'd done it.''

"That's about the way we'd figured it out," said Calhoun gently. "You'll have to come along with us now, you know."

Tucker stood up stiffly. "I know." On the ride up to the jail he didn't say any more. They booked him in, and the jailer took his belt, the little money on him, a pocket knife, left him cigarettes and lighter. Back in the car Calhoun said, "And if ever a man had provocation—they may reduce the charge.''

"Very possibly, under the circumstances," said Mendoza. "And for once I can't say I'd be sorry."

At the office they found Palliser and Grace in and told them about it. Palliser said, "Well, I will be damned. I'd have bet money on Lopez. And that alibi—I don't think it crossed anybody's mind that there could be a hole in it. That was good thinking, Pat.''

"You know," said Calhoun, "I think he was ready to talk about it, he might have come in to confess even if we hadn't gone back to question him. He's an ordinary decent man, not a natural killer.''

"And what have you been accomplishing?" Mendoza asked Palliser.

"These damned kids," said Palliser. He sat down at his desk and massaged the back of his neck wearily. "They're dried out now and Wanda and I've been talking to them with some Juvenile officers. And thank God it's Juvenile's headache. They'll be taking a look at the parents, and deciding if they're fit or unfit. We didn't have any trouble getting the story out of them. The Jenkins woman seems to have been a decent sort too. She'd tried to get the girl off drugs and the girl resented being bossed around, she called it. Sunday night this Tommy and his sister—he's Tommy Valdez—came by to see the girl and they started playing records, and Mrs. Jenkins told them to turn the volume down. Tommy was strung out on reefers, and he carries a switchblade—he just knifed her to shut her up. Then they were on their own, nobody to order them around, so the girl took all the cash in her mother's handbag and they bought some more reefers and the uppers and downers, and got all the other kids in and had the hell of a party."

"*¡Vaya por Dios!*" said Mendoza.

"Juvenile's welcome to them." Palliser was looking tired. "All we have to do is submit the lab evidence for the hearing."

The phone rang in Mendoza's office and they all trailed after him in case it was a new call.

It was Dr. Bainbridge in the coroner's office. "This is a slightly offbeat one, Mendoza, and I thought you'd like to know about it right away. I'll send the report over when I've written it."

"Yes, doctor, go ahead." Mendoza punched the amplifier and Bainbridge's voice came loud and clear into the office.

"This Carlos Avila, an apparent homicide victim last Sunday. We get a little busy here and I just got to him a while ago. I hope you haven't arrested anybody for killing him."

"We were waiting to hear what you had to say, doctor."

"Well, don't," said Bainbridge. "He died a natural death, and rather a funny one."

"*¿Cómo?* What killed him?"

"A cerebral hemorrhage," said Bainbridge. "I'd have a guess that when he died he was mad about something."

"That's what we heard. He'd just had a little traffic accident and he was cussing out the fellow who caused it."

"That figures," said Bainbridge. "The hemorrhage was caused by an aneurysm bursting in the section of the brain called the Circle of Willis. It ruptured because he was in a rage and his blood pressure was up."

"Now that is a funny one," said Mendoza. "Thanks, doctor." He put the phone down. "So Shaver's off the hook, and so much for the eyewitnesses—¡Ca!" Three men had sworn that Shaver had hit Avila and knocked him down, and Shaver was telling the truth when he said he'd been five feet away from him.

Nobody had found Scott and Cooper yet. The rest of the men in heard about Tucker and they talked about that for a while, and then Landers brought in a suspect for questioning and Galeano sat in on that.

Nothing went down for the night watch until nearly ten o'clock, and the call was to a movie house on North Main. It was Schenke's night off, and Conway and Piggott both went out on it. The shabby old theater ran exclusively Spanish-language films. There were two men waiting for them, Antonio Chavez and Bernardo Mercado. Chavez was the ticket collector, Mercado the manager. They both spoke good English.

"It was just after the last show began," said Chavez. "Nine-thirty that'd be. Elena, that's the girl in the ticket booth, she'd just left, closed down the booth, and I'd collected the tickets from all the customers, there's not much of a crowd, and I was just about to take off too. Last thing I had to do was lock the front doors inside. And then this dude shows up, he came in the front door with a gun. He says I should take him to the manager's office, so I did. Mr. Mercado, Elena'd given him the money bag and he was counting the take."

"So I could tell you what he got," said Mercado. "Damn it, the first time we've ever been held up. It was sixty-four dollars and seventy-five cents, business is always slow in the middle of the week."

"Can you describe him?" asked Conway.

They both gave the same description, a man in the late twenties, thin, dark complexion and dark hair. "But another thing I can tell you about him," said Chavez, "and maybe Mr. Mercado noticed

130

it too, he had a scar on his hand. Not his gun hand, his left hand. I saw it when he took the bag of money, he told Mr. Mercado to put it all back in the bag and he reached for it."

"I saw it too," said Mercado.

"What kind of scar?" asked Piggott.

"From an old burn," said Chavez. "It wasn't fresh, he isn't going to lose it. My kid brother got a bad burn on his arm years ago, and this looked just the same, kind of puckered and lighter than the rest of the skin."

"Well, that may be a help in locating him," said Conway. "We'd like you both to come in and make statements about this tomorrow."

Bill Moss was at the intersection of Third and Hoover when he got a 459 call. It was five minutes past two. He let out a few choice expletives when he heard the address. That damned place again, but they couldn't just let it go and forget about it. This time it might be real. He swung the squad in a U-turn, and put in a call for a backup. When he got up to the high school, he waited five minutes for Sanchez to show.

"Listen, this is getting to be a goddamned nuisance," said Sanchez.

"Tell the Board of Education," said Moss.

They went round the place, checked all the doors and windows, and found everything peaceful. They found the security guard asleep in his car again, and woke him up to let them in. When he unlocked the box covering the burglar alarm system, two dead mice fell out.

"They've got to do something about this," said Sanchez loudly. "We don't get paid to deal with mice, for God's sake!"

But it had all taken some time, checking the building. When Moss got back to the spot on his regular tour where he'd been when he got the call, it was nearly an hour later. When he got up midway in the next block on Hoover, he saw a man lying on the sidewalk, by the fitful light of the street lamp there. He slid the squad into the curb and got out to see if the man was drunk or dead. He put the

131

flashlight on him. He was a stocky bald man in the mid-fifties, and Moss knew him. He was the night bartender at this place right here, and his name was O'Shea; he was just outside the door of the bar. Moss had been chased down here a few times to deal with the obstreperous customers and a couple of brawls.

O'Shea had a faint pulse but he looked bad. And Moss knew just when it had happened, the coronary or stroke or whatever it was. O'Shea would have closed the bar down at two A.M., and he'd have just come out, on his way to his car to go home, when it had hit him. The night's take would be in the little safe behind the bar. O'Shea had told him about that, the owner of the place picked it up every morning. He'd have just stepped out the door when whatever it was had hit him. And if it hadn't been for that damn phony 459 call, Moss would have come along here and spotted him two minutes later.

He put in a call for the paramedics and went back to O'Shea. Just before the ambulance got there he lost the pulse.

The paramedics got him inside and tried the electric shocks on him, but it was no go. "If we'd got to him sooner," said one of them, "just after it hit him, we could probably have brought him back."

Moss had rather liked O'Shea, who'd been a tough honest man. He'd told Moss once that he had a son on the Fresno department. "Goddamn those goddamned mice!" said Moss savagely, and the paramedics looked at him as if he was crazy.

Patrolman Desmond Hatfield, cruising down Western Avenue in Gardena, was automatically checking every public and private parking lot on his beat, looking at plate numbers. He was also taking a look at every car parked in the street.

That patrolman shot and killed had belonged to Central beat, but he'd been an L.A.P.D. man and every man on the force was hot to get the killer. The killer was tied to this Nevada plate number, and at the briefing they'd all been told that it was slightly more possible that he might show up somewhere in Seventy-seventh Street Division territory than anywhere else.

About nine o'clock Hatfield turned into a public lot. It was alongside one of the gambling houses. He ambled up the first aisle, looking at plate numbers; he had memorized that Nevada plate. And by God, in the middle of the second aisle, there it was as big as life—the old Buick with that Nevada plate. Exultation surged through his veins, and he grabbed the mike. "I've got Carpenter's car right in front of me, send me some backup."

The backup arrived within five minutes, Durwood and Hernandez in two squads. The first place to check was the card parlor, and they went in there. They all knew that photo by heart, the long rather handsome face, the dark hair, wide-set eyes under straight bushy eyebrows: They knew the official description, six feet, a hundred and sixty.

There was the usual crowd at the tables, a couple of waiters scurrying around with drinks. They fanned out to look, and inevitably the uniforms aroused some interest, but it couldn't be helped. Two minutes later Durwood rejoined Hatfield and said, "The table against the wall. It's him."

It was. There were five men sitting there, and a good-looking dark girl sitting beside the table looking on at the game. They all went up there, and Hatfield said, "Jerome Carpenter?"

He looked up automatically, and then his expression froze. They all had their guns out. They knew he had a gun. "On your feet," said Hatfield, "and don't try anything. You're under arrest."

He stood up slowly. The other men were just looking startled. The girl jumped up and said in a loud voice, "What are you arresting him for? His name's not Carpenter—"

Durwood got the cuffs on him. He just stood there woodenly. "What are you arresting him for?" she demanded hysterically.

The briefing hadn't said anything about a possible girl. "For murder," said Hatfield. "He shot a cop last week."

And she said, quick and defensive, "I didn't know anything about it till the shot woke me up. I didn't know. You can't say I had anything to do with it."

So of course they took her in as an accessory.

Chapter 8

Schenke had called Mendoza at home last night, getting the word from Seventy-seventh Street. The men who'd brought Carpenter in had found the gun in the glove compartment of the Buick. Mendoza and Higgins went over to the jail as soon as they got in that morning.

The jailer brought Carpenter up to one of the interrogation rooms. "We won't waste much time on you," said Mendoza coldly, "but we'd be interested to know just why you shot the cop."

Carpenter was looking sullen. He leaned back in the hard chair and said, "For God's sake, it was just a stupid accident, that was all! Because I don't know the damned town. Maria, she'd had a couple drinks too many, she was asleep in the back of the car, we were on the way home from one of the card rooms down there, and I got confused at that place they call the Stack where the freeways come together. I got shunted onto an off ramp and I didn't know where the hell I was. Then the cop stopped me, and asked for my license, and like a damned fool—I realized it the minute I'd done it—I gave him my own license instead of Andy's."

"Andy Dickinson," said Higgins. "Who is he?"

"We were in the Army together, in the same barracks. When I took off I took his billfold, I figured I'd need a Social Security card to get a job, the Army'd trace me if I used my own, I had all his

134

stuff, but I'd handed the cop my own license."

"Where did you get the gun?" asked Mendoza.

"That was Andy's too, I had it on the seat beside me, just for protection. I didn't know I was going to shoot the damn cop till I did it. It was just a kind of stupid mistake. And then Maria woke up and I just took off."

They didn't talk to him much longer. He said he and the girl had been staying at a motel in Monterey Park. Over in Vegas he'd won a stake of nearly twelve thousand bucks at poker, and he said bitterly, "I should have stayed there, but I'd never been to L.A. and I come over just to look around."

They didn't bother to talk to the girl at all; she'd been transferred to the Sybil Brand Institute.

"Just for nothing," said Higgins heavily. "He was afraid the Army would catch up to him when the police had his valid license, with his real name on it. Stupid you can say, Luis. He drove off and left the license in Gunther's hand."

Mendoza said, "It's the stupidities we're dealing with mostly, George." But at least they'd caught up to him, and this would be Murder One.

There were ongoing things to work. On that heist at the theater last night, Palliser had gone down to R. and I. with the description, and the computer had turned up a name, Ernest Wade. He had one count of armed robbery, and he was the only one in the files with that mark on him, the old burn scar on the back of his left hand. He had served a little over a year in, and was off parole since four months ago. He fitted the description otherwise. There wasn't, of course, any current address. Palliser went back to the office and called Welfare and Rehab. Wade's P.A. officer was surprised to be asked about him. "I'd be sorry to hear he backslid, Sergeant, I thought he was a good type, really meant to straighten out. I got him a job at a parking lot at a restaurant in Hollywood, I thought he was doing all right. He was living in a little apartment in Hollywood." He gave Palliser both addresses. Palliser tried them both. Wade had left the Hollywood apartment, and nobody there knew where he'd moved. At the restaurant, the other lot attendant said,

135

"Ernie quit here a couple of months ago, he got a better job over in Pasadena, he's driving a cab for Yellow."

He could be traced through the cab company. The heat was still building up. Palliser started for Pasadena resignedly.

The man turned into wolf had been at work all day, but not working as quickly as usual or as carefully. His mind kept turning from the figures before him now and then. He was bent over the calculator but not using it, and he started when the man at the next desk spoke. "If I only knew what?" he asked.

"I beg your pardon?"

"Well, you just said it, if I only knew, and you had a funny look on your face."

"Did I really? I don't know what I could have meant, I'm afraid I'm getting absentminded," and he managed a laugh. But he was suddenly afraid, conscious of the new awful temptation in him, the Voice now whispering new things to him. Nobody must ever find out or he would be stopped from reaching the ecstasy; but the Voice was whispering insidiously, that they should know, the world should know that he was a man of superior understanding, different and superior to other men, he should tell the world about himself. He was feeling afraid and confused. He had always obeyed the Voice, but he was afraid of what other men would do to him if they knew about him. But there was the awful new temptation to shout it aloud to the world, his discovery of the ecstasy of the blood. As he bent over the calculator again his hands were trembling.

About two o'clock on Thursday afternoon Landers and Galeano, trying that rooming house on Magnolia Street again, found Ron Scott and Joe Cooper at home. They brought them back to headquarters for questioning. Scott was medium black, Cooper darker, and they were just what Landers and Galeano might have expected, the very typical stupid punks. They were surprised at cops coming after them, and did some cussing.

136

Landers and Galeano took them back down the hall and planted them in an interrogation room.

"About that break-in at the house on Crandall Street," said Galeano conversationally. "The old lady can identify you both, you know." Scott and Cooper just glowered. "We know it was you two pulled that job, stabbed the old lady when she found you there. That wasn't very smart, you might have killed her. She'll take one look at you and say it was you two, and you're both up for assault."

"Oh, hell," said Scott. "I didn't mean assault nobody, we was just scared. We didn't know nobody was to home there. We rang the bell and nobody answered so we figured nobody was to home." The deaf old lady in bed without her hearing aid, thought Landers. "Then all of a sudden she come out and turns on a light, and we was scared. I just cut her a little so we could get away. How'd you know it was us?"

They both felt tired looking at the typical stupid louts. "Because we're smarter than you," said Landers, and out of curiosity asked Scott, "Why did you take a bath? We understand you don't do that very often."

Scott said, "Well, goddamn, it was an awful hot night and I didn't have no shirt on and I got the old lady's blood all over me."

"Oh, for God's sake," said Galeano. They took them over to the jail and booked them in. "It does make you wonder about that girl," said Landers. "I wonder if she'll ante up bail for Scott again."

Palliser talked to the Pasadena dispatcher of the Yellow Cab Company, after he'd stopped for lunch. "Yeah, Wade," said the dispatcher, "he's been on the job a couple of months, I think he's on a run right now, what in hell do the cops want with him? Is he in any trouble?"

"Maybe," said Palliser. "I'd like you to call him in."

The dispatcher shrugged, and got on the radio.

137

Palliser went out to the big parking lot and waited, and half an hour later Ernest Wade showed up in a Yellow Cab. Palliser said, "Wade?" and showed him the badge.

He was a rather good-looking young man, neatly dressed. He said, "What's it about? The dispatcher just said, a cop. What do you want with me? I haven't done anything."

"There was a heist downtown last night," said Palliser. "And both the witnesses described you, they noticed the scar on your hand." It was a noticeable scar, puckered and ugly.

"That's not so," said Wade. "I never did a thing like that, it wasn't me. Whatever anybody says. I've been straight now, I'll never do anything against the law again, sir, honest. I got in with some bad kids when I was just a kid myself, I fooled around some with the dope and all, and I pulled that job, held up that drugstore, and I did the time for it, but that's all behind me. While I was in the joint, the Reverend Jones, he made me see the light, he's the chaplain there and he brought me to God. I'll never do another wrong thing the rest of my life. I've got all straightened out with God and I'll stay that way."

"Very commendable," said Palliser. "Where were you between eight and ten last night?"

"I was at church," said Wade. "The Church of the Brethren here in town, I was at choir practice. The Reverend Wagner and everybody else can tell you that. There's about twenty of us in the choir and the organist, Mrs. Blake."

Palliser shut his eyes for a moment. So all the legwork was for nothing, and now there was nowhere else to go on that heist, Wade had been the only one in the files with such a scar. But it was gratifying to know that at least one ex-con had got straightened out. He said, "Sorry to have bothered you," and then he thought about Tucker's alibi. He wasted a little more time looking up that church, locating the minister. The minister confirmed Wade's alibi, and Palliser started back downtown. At least they'd caught up to Carpenter, which was also gratifying.

* * *

138

When Phil had gone on maternity leave, she and Landers had had the same day off, Saturday. Now that she was back to work, she was off on Thursdays. Landers had just got back to his desk at three o'clock after sitting in on questioning a heist suspect with Galeano when his phone rang. He picked it up and said, "Landers."

"Tom," said Phil excitedly, "I had to call you right away, you won't believe it but we've sold the house!"

"No," said Landers, "don't tell me. I thought we'd be stuck with that place until the baby was grown up."

"Well, the realtor had to lower the price but that doesn't matter, just so long as we're out from under," said Phil. "It's a couple, the man's just got a new job here, and they just love to paint and redecorate and remodel, they couldn't stop talking about all they're going to do to it. And it'll be a thirty-day escrow, they got a loan from the bank right away, all the paperwork's going on right now."

"Well, praise be," said Landers fervently. "Now we start looking for an apartment somewhere closer in, and depending on the rent, maybe we can get you fixed up with a car."

"It was like a miracle," said Phil. "I thought we'd be stuck with it forever too."

"Tell you what," said Landers, "you get all dressed up and I'll take you out to dinner to celebrate."

"That's a deal," said Phil happily.

The night watch sat around until eight-thirty, when a call came in to an assault. Conway and Schenke went out on it; the address was on Virgil. They got there at the same time as the ambulance, and followed the paramedics up the stairs in the old apartment building. In the hall outside an open apartment door, there were seven or eight people standing around and the patrolman, Carlson, had a man in cuffs. A woman was lying on the living-room floor unconscious. The paramedics took her off in a hurry, and Conway asked, "What's the story?"

Carlson said, "He was beating the hell out of her, the neighbors called in." The man sitting on the couch was a big burly man with

139

a barrel chest. He looked about thirty. He had reddish-brown hair and a pugnacious jaw. He wasn't saying anything. They went out to the hall and talked to the neighbors.

"It was terrible," said a fat woman in a blue bathrobe. "All the screams, and him yelling swearwords. I'm the one called the police."

One of the men said, "Nobody knows their name, they just moved in here last week. He might have killed the poor woman, my God. She was begging him to stop beating her."

Back in the apartment Conway asked, "What's your name?"

He said sullenly, "Ayers, Jack Ayers."

"That's your wife? Why were you beating her?"

"That's my business."

He wouldn't say anything else. They sent him over to the jail with Carlson, and went out to the Emergency wing to find out how the woman was. After twenty minutes or so an intern came out to them and said, "She isn't going to die, but she's pretty damn well worked over. Couple of broken ribs, broken arm, and a fractured jaw."

"My God," said Conway, "I wonder why he was so mad at her."

"She's not able to talk," said the intern. "That jaw. She's still unconscious anyway, you can't talk to her. And does it matter? It was the husband? Maybe she didn't have dinner ready on time, or was nagging him about something."

Probably it didn't matter, but Conway was curious and it ought to go in the report. They went over to the jail. Ayers was sitting in the detention room, the cuffs removed. "You feel like saying anything now?" asked Schenke. "Why in hell were you beating your wife like that? You came within an ace of killing her."

Ayers looked at them and there was still red fury possessing him. He said in a rough voice, "Wife! Some wife! Jesus Christ, we only been married a week and I thought everything was fine, and then she—*she*!—tonight I find out about it, for God's sake, it isn't she no ways, just a goddamn fag, and I don't want nothin' to do with queers! Tellin' me, one of these goddamned sex-change

140

operations, she—he—it had been a man, always wanted to be a girl and had this goddamned operation— I don't know what they do, cut everything off I guess—she sure acted like a girl, but it's just a damn fag, and I like to throwed up, I found out. I was so damned mad I coulda done murder—I can't be legal married to a fag, can I?''

With a straight face Conway said, ''Well, legally she's a female now, Ayers.'' Ayers grunted.

''I don't have no truck with queers, goddamn it. Trickin' me like that, I ought to have killed her—him—it! How long do I have to stay in jail?''

''I couldn't say,'' said Schenke. ''She may want to charge you with aggravated assault, or even attempted homicide.'' He just grunted again.

Outside they began to laugh. ''You can see it would have been a shock to him,'' said Schenke.

''And he's a big tough he-man,'' said Conway. ''His macho image outraged. But of all the funny things, Bob—'' They went back to the office to write a report on it.

Mendoza came into the office with Hackett and Higgins a little early. Farrell was already sitting on the switchboard, and said, ''The jail's been trying to get you, Lieutenant.''

''Oh? Well, put a call through.'' Mendoza went back to his office.

When the call came through, it was the chief jailer. He said, ''I'm sorry as hell, Lieutenant, but we've lost a prisoner for you. You know all the precautions we take, try to prevent possible suicides, but sometimes it happens anyway.''

''Who?'' asked Mendoza.

''That Samuel Tucker. He must have been damned determined to do it. He waited until the regular inspection had been made at midnight, climbed up on his cot and unscrewed the light bulb, smashed it and used the biggest piece to slash his wrists. The jailer in that wing never found him until the next inspection about two A.M., and raised the alarm, but he was too far gone.''

141

"Por Dios, that poor devil," said Mendoza. "Determined you can say, that took some nerve. Do you know if he called anybody when he was booked in?" Tucker had mentioned a family.

"Yeah, his father, he came to see him yesterday. No, I don't know any address."

The family ought to be informed. Mendoza passed that on to the rest of them, and Grace said, "The clearing-up to do. I'll see what I can find out. There may be an address book at the house." He went out.

The D.A.'s office called to say that Calhoun's hearing on that shooting was scheduled for Tuesday, and Calhoun did some cussing about it. "It would be my day off, of course."

Mendoza passed around the night report, and they all had a little laugh about Ayers. "There's nowhere else to go on that theater heist," said Palliser, "Wade being cleared. And it's a piddling little thing, sixty-five bucks and nobody hurt."

Wanda was down in Juvenile on that business of the kids. There were still a couple of heisters to look for, and it was Galeano's day off. The day dragged on with no new calls, until after four o'clock, when Farrell gave them a new homicide. Calhoun and Hackett went out to look at it.

And the crime rate was up all over, on every type of crime, but this kind of thing could still raise their blood pressure, happening in broad daylight in the middle of the big city. The body was lying on the sidewalk in front of an independent pharmacy on Beverly Boulevard, the body of an elderly man in gray slacks and a white shirt. The patrolman was Gibson. There was another man there, a thin middle-aged man in a white smock, looking distressed. "It's Mr. Hagen," he said. "He'd just been in to get his wife's prescription refilled—the Synthroid. They just live up on Rosemont, a couple of blocks. He hadn't been gone but a couple of minutes when I went up front to straighten out the magazines, and I heard a little commotion out here, I looked, and there are two black fellows roughing him up. I saw him knocked down, one of them going through his pockets—and I yelled at them and came out, but they were already taking off— I don't know if they killed him or if he might have had a heart attack—"

Hackett looked at the body, lifted the head and felt it. "Probably a fractured skull when he fell on the sidewalk," he said.

"But there are usually people on the street," said the pharmacist. "Just not wanting to get involved, or maybe I was the only one who saw it, I don't know."

And there was a muffled scream from behind them, and they turned. "What's happened to Carl?" She was a plump old lady in a cotton housedress. "Oh, what's happened? I remembered I'd forgot to ask him—get a quart of ice cream—and I came—"

"It's his wife," said the pharmacist agitatedly. "They live up on Rosemont— I'm afraid he's dead, Mrs. Hagen—" She went on her knees beside the body, too shocked to begin to cry. "Some men were robbing him, they knocked him down—"

In the suddenness of her shock, she seized on the irrelevant, and she looked up at the pharmacist and said, "But where is his necktie?—somebody stole his necktie, and he was so proud of it— our daughter gave it to him for his birthday, and it's got all the grandchildren's names embroidered on it—we've got five grandchildren, you know—Janice, Billie, Gary, Linda, Michelle—" She was still repeating that like a litany when she began to sob.

Calhoun and Hackett took her home, which was a little house a block away on Rosemont, and Calhoun called the daughter. She lived in South Pasadena and said she'd come right down.

"Broad daylight," said Hackett. "A main drag. It happens too often."

Jim Myers was moving that night. He didn't have much to move, but he was annoyed about it. He'd been living in a two-room apartment on Lake Street and the rent had gone up. He was twenty-three and just had a job as a stock clerk at a market, but he was studying accounting by a correspondence course at night and meant to do a lot better someday. He'd found another two-room apartment for the same rent he'd been paying, over on Maryland,

143

and when he got off work at eight, he got all his possessions into the old heap of a car he was driving. He didn't have much. All his clothes in two suitcases went into the trunk, and aside from that he just had a few odds and ends of dishes, tableware, a couple of pots and pans. It was a nuisance cooking for himself, but it was too expensive to eat out very often. The last thing, he dumped the contents of the two kitchen drawers into a cardboard carton, and that went on the front seat. He handed over the key to the manager and thought he'd stop for a beer and a substantial sandwich somewhere. He'd had the sandwich and was sitting over another beer when the girl came up to his table and sat down. "You like to buy me a drink?" she asked in a friendly voice.

He sized her up. She was pretty cute with blond hair. Suddenly he began to feel a lot better. Hell, he thought, a guy's got to have some fun sometimes. "Sure," he said. She was sizing him up too.

When she was halfway through with her drink, he asked bluntly, "What's the price?"

She giggled and said, "Twenty-five."

It was a little money, but he hadn't had a girl in a while and she was cute. "Okay," he said, "come on, you tell me where to go."

She got into the car with him and said, "You go straight up and turn on Fourth."

He started the car and turned out into traffic.

"What's in the box, lover?" she asked.

"Nothing much," said Myers absently.

Nosily she opened the top and reached inside. The first thing she brought out was a little meat cleaver and the second thing was a long butcher knife. She opened her mouth and started to scream like a siren going off. "You're him—you're the monster—oh, God, let me out of here—" She clawed at the door handle and got the door open. Startled, Myers braked, and she nearly fell out of the car, and ran screaming up to the sidewalk and back down the street.

Myers stared after her, completely mystified. Women!, he thought. You never could figure out what got into them.

He didn't read anything in the papers except the sports section, and he'd never heard of the monster killing the females.

On Saturday night the night watch left them a heist at a market, at closing time at ten o'clock. There had been five witnesses, and they'd all be coming in to make statements and look at mug shots. Which would give the day men something to do. Yesterday Grace had located Tucker's parents from an address book at the duplex, but they hadn't been home; it was a house in Hollywood. Today he tried again to break the bad news, and found them at home. Mrs. Tucker burst into sobs. "It was that girl, I never liked that girl, the first time I saw her I knew she was a bad lot—"

Tucker said heavily, "You couldn't get us yesterday because we were talking to a lawyer, hiring a lawyer for him." There wasn't much to say to them.

When Grace got back to the office, Galeano and Palliser had taken the witnesses down to look at mug shots. One of the squads called in a dead body, and Higgins went to look at it, but it wouldn't give them any more work. It was the body of an elderly man in an alley off Alvarado, not a mark on him and nothing in his shabby clothes but a half bottle of cheap muscatel. He was probably another derelict dead of natural causes.

The witnesses all agreed on one mug shot, couldn't pick out the second heister. His name was Alberto Cruz and he had the right pedigree for it, one charge of armed robbery, but there wasn't any current address.

Galeano called his former parole officer, who said, "Well, I'm afraid I can't help you. He was working at a gas station while he was on P.A., but I'd suspect as soon as he didn't have to see me regularly he'd quit. You can try it, of course," and he named the station. They tried it, but Cruz had quit the job three months ago, it was another dead end. There was a car registered to him and they put out an A.P.B. on it.

The twins had probably never heard of the Chinese water torture, but they had adopted the principle instinctively. Every time they were within speaking distance of their parents, the subject came unerringly back to the swimming pool.

"And we know just where it ought to be," said Johnny, hanging onto Mendoza's arm as he tried to finish his drink. "Right the other side of the pony ring—"

"And we could have pretty green tiles," said Terry happily, "and nice little tables with umbrellas over them—like at the place the lady wouldn't let us stay."

"I said no," said Mendoza firmly. "No swimming pool. You just put it out of your minds and forget it."

"Now you heard what your father said," said Alison. "Let's hear no more about it."

That fell on deaf ears, of course. "We could have a raft to paddle," said Terry, bouncing excitedly.

"And we could teach Cedric to swim!" said Johnny.

"Por la gracia de Dios," said Alison. "I could murder that Coatesworth woman!"

At nine-forty the night watch got called out to a heist, and Conway took it with Piggott. It was a liquor store on Olympic, and the owner had been just about to close at nine o'clock when the pair came in. The patrolman was Powell, and he said, "I called an ambulance first, he was bleeding pretty bad. This is Mr. Fontana."

"But she shot Al! She just shot him! I still don't believe it—they were just kids, just young kids, seventeen, eighteen—she had a great big gun—they come in, I'm thinking I'll have to ask I.D., prove they're not minors, and then she pulls out the gun—and you got a picture of her! The officer here, he shows me a picture of her—" the artist's sketch of the gorgeous redhead. "Yes, yes, she's got all this bright red hair, I didn't believe it— I couldn't tell you anything about the boy—she says, it's a stickup and clean out the register, and I don't believe it and I guess neither did Al."

"Al who?" asked Piggott.

"Al Flores, he's my clerk—he didn't open the register and she waved the gun at him and says, I mean business, mister, hurry it up, and when he couldn't open it right away—we'd been having trouble

146

with it sticking—she shot him! That gun went off like a cannon! And I got the register open and gave her all the bills and they went out."

"Did you follow them to see if they got into a car?" asked Conway, knowing the answer.

"I did not. I was too worried about Al. I called the police, I'm just about to call an ambulance when the officer came. Has that girl held up other people? Just a young girl, for God's sake—"

It was a replay of all the other jobs Bonnie and Clyde had pulled, and offered no new leads. Conway and Piggott told Fontana to come in tomorrow and make a statement, and they went out to the Emergency wing to see if they now had a homicide. The doctor they talked to said, "Well, he could be worse. The slug's in his chest, looks as if it may have just missed the heart. We won't try to get it out until we pump some blood into him and he's out of shock."

"When you do get it out," said Piggott, "we'll want it for comparison."

"Probably sometime tomorrow," said the doctor.

"That pair," said Conway on the way back to the office. "That damned pair. Sooner or later that redhead will end up killing somebody. And if she's such a gorgeous chick as that sketch suggests—and the red hair—you'd have thought one of the Traffic men would have spotted her by now. I know, don't say it, we're spread pretty thin and it's a big town. God, I'll be glad to get home tonight."

Piggott yawned and said, "So will I. At least I'll say one thing, the baby's stopped waking us up at four A.M. I thought for a while she never would, but Prudence says they grow out of it, and she did."

"And thank God I'm a carefree bachelor," said Conway.

The man turned into wolf had been on the prowl again, and now he was sensuously satiated. He stood at the doorway of the small shabby apartment, taking a last lingering look at what he was leaving behind. He had taken a long warm shower in the bathroom and gotten dressed again, and he was ready to leave.

147

He had his hand on the doorknob when he heard the woman's high heels making little taps on the bare floor of the hall, and then the knock at the door. He stood still.

"Gloria? Gloria, I know you're there, you'd better open up." After a moment the voice rose sharper and higher. "Gloria, you know damned well I'm not going to forget about that twenty you owe me! You better pay up right quick, or I'll tell Jake and he'll work you over some so the johns won't think you're such a bargain. You hear me?"

The man inside the door was seized with a terrible, nearly irresistible temptation to open the door, to say, Come in and see what Gloria looks like now. He remained motionless, and heard the high heels click away down the hall. Presently he opened the door. The hall was empty and quiet. He closed the door behind him and went rapidly down the stairs and into the street.

Mendoza wouldn't be in until later, on Sunday morning. The day men swore, reading about the latest hit by Bonnie and Clyde. Palliser called the hospital to ask about Flores, and the doctor said they were just going after the slug. "You can send somebody over to get it in an hour."

"And it'll be another slug out of that same cannon," said Landers, "and no damn leads on it at all. Maybe we've been a little slow on this, John. Look what the boss turned up from the N.C.I.C. hot line. Could be if we ask, this pair had been operating in somebody else's territory before they landed here. Minors be damned, if they have, somebody ought to remember the redhead."

"And even if that's so," said Calhoun, "I don't suppose anybody else'd have any leads on them either. As far as I can see, our only hope of dropping on them is that sketch."

Sometime they should check on the Ayers woman who'd got beaten up the other night, see if she wanted to charge the husband with assault with intent; that would make the charge a little heavier. And this coming week, there'd be indictments to cover in court—Carpenter, the bank heisters Price and Unger, Juan Diaz.

148

The lab report and autopsy report on the Metzger woman would be coming in. Number forty-two. And there would be new calls going down. Hopefully, the A.P.B. on Alberto Cruz would turn him up. The P.A. man had said he hadn't any family here, and he hadn't known of any close friends.

Mendoza came in about eleven and said, "I don't give a damn whether there's any work to do or not, I think I'll sit in the office all day just for some peace and quiet. *Demonios,* that pair of twin monsters can't talk about anything but the pretty swimming pool, and I refuse to even think about it. That damned place has run into enough money as it is, what with the fence and the electric gate and the apartment for the Kearneys, not to mention the ponies and the sheep, and on this I put my foot down."

"That's what you get for turning into a respectable married man," said Higgins, laughing.

Galeano brought back the slug from the hospital and dropped it off at the lab.

"And we've got the confession from Scott," said Hackett, "but I suppose it'll be just as well to ask Mrs. Ryerson to identify them." He called the hospital; she had been discharged. "The daughter was coming, she's probably with her at the house." He looked up the number and dialed, and talked to the daughter. Mrs. Ryerson thought she'd feel well enough to come in tomorrow, so Hackett called the jail to arrange a lineup. Scott and Cooper would be getting indicted this week too, and there'd be the autopsy report on Carl Hagen, but there was nothing to do about that one.

At four o'clock they got an urgent call to some mayhem. There seemed to have been a wholesale battle going on down on Twenty-third Street, with six squads sent out and some dead bodies. They all went out on it, and it was going to make some overtime.

There were four bodies, one black, three Latin, all shot, and a whole crowd of witnesses, some of them the honest citizens.

"All those boys," said one of those, who ran a snack bar across the street, "they're Caballeros. They're mean and tough, we all steer clear of 'em."

149

The gang members, the five left alive, were voluble and defensive. "They just come in and start shootin'—they was all from the Black Colonels, we know 'em—they mean and bad, man, we didn't do nothin'. They say we ripped off their van, stole some reefers, but we never—they shoot Bernie and Al right off, and we go for guns, we gotta protect ourselves, and Tony got one of 'em but then the big guy with the patch, he got Tony—"

It was going to be quite a thing to sort out. The Latin victims and immediate witnesses were all members of the Caballeros gang, and if there was always rivalry and resentment between the gangs, between the blacks and the Latins it was never-ending war. This was the main hangout of the Caballeros, a garage on Twenty-third Street. The gangs usually dealt in the drugs; and by what they could gather, the black gang-members had gotten the idea that the Caballeros had swiped some of their supply and were taking consequent vengeance. They took all the witnesses, guilty and innocent, back to the office for questioning, and of course they just heard the same monotonous answers from the gang members. The other gang, the Black Colonels, had been dispersing as the squads started to arrive, some honest citizen down there calling police.

Mendoza left the rest of them getting statements as best they could, and went up to the Narco office. He nodded at Henry Glasser, who was talking to a citizen in the big office, and marched into Callaghan's office without knocking. "And what the hell are you doing here?" asked Callaghan. "I'm just about to go home, it's the end of the day."

"Maybe you're not," said Mendoza. "We've got something on hand." He told Callaghan about it. "They're not very coherent, but we've got one description, a big black fellow wearing a patch over one eye." Narco had more dealings with the gangs than Robbery-Homicide.

Callaghan ran his fingers through hair as red as Alison's and said instantly, "Charlie Webb. He had that eye gouged out by a knife about two years back, in a rumble with another Latin gang down in Seventy-seventh Street territory. Nobody got charged on it. The Black Colonels are a dangerous bunch, Luis."

150

"We've applied for a search warrant for that garage. By the time we got there, only one gun visible, on one corpse. We'd like to find the rest of them. Evidently the Caballeros aren't practiced marksmen, they don't seem to have got but one of the Colonels. We don't know who he is yet."

"And you'll probably come across some of the dope there," said Callaghan.

"That's the only description we've got, but it's definite that Webb shot at least one of them. Have you got an address for him?"

"Are you kidding?" said Callaghan. "He's served little stretches for dealing, but we haven't had him in for about a year. He lives on and off with one of the girls belonging to the gang." The girls were usually held in common. "None of that kind live anywhere very long, they move around. Your best bet is to stake out their main headquarters, it's a garage on Union. He'll show there sooner or later. But let me know what you pick up at that place."

It got to be after seven; Mendoza had called Alison, and none of them had had dinner. The night watch was helping out on talking to witnesses. There'd be a lot of paperwork on this one.

The search warrant came through, and Mendoza, Hackett, Higgins, and Grace went out to ransack that garage. They found four handguns, a lot of ammo, a generous supply of marijuana joints, and a small stash of cocaine in one of the pickup trucks in the garage, so Mendoza called Narco and a couple of their night men came out. They went back to the office at nine o'clock, dropping the evidence at the lab. They looked in at the Robbery-Homicide office briefly and then headed for home.

"I am beat," said Hackett as they waited for the elevator. "What a day. We'll pick up Webb eventually, and he'll get charged with manslaughter and spend a year in. What the hell, that kind we've got with us forever, and nobody'll ever change them." The elevator arrived and Schenke got out of it with a big young black man.

"New call?" said Mendoza.

"He got into a fight over a girl at a dancehall down on Venice, and stuck a knife into him. It's just assault, the fellow isn't dead."

They glanced at the man as Schenke led him toward the Robbery-Homicide office, and got into the elevator.

But as Mendoza reached to punch the ground-floor button, Hackett said suddenly, "Hold it. There's something I want to check." He went back to the office.

Schenke was just on the way to an interrogation room with his capture, and Hackett went after them into the little square room. "What's his name?" he asked Schenke.

"Adam Scofield." Schenke looked a little surprised.

Hackett looked at Scofield. He was very nattily dressed in a bright blue suit, white shirt, and tie. It was the tie that had caught Hackett's eye, a royal-blue tie with names embroidered all over it in red. He asked, "Where'd you get that tie?"

"None of your business, man," said Scofield, but he looked surprised.

"Take it off," said Hackett. "Let's see it."

Reluctantly, Scofield removed the tie and handed it over. The embroidery was in red, and consisted of five names, repeated at various angles—Janice, Billie, Gary, Linda, Michelle. Hackett felt warm satisfaction and also complete astonishment. "You took this off the old man you and a pal of yours mugged on the street. For God's sake, why?"

"You're crazy, man. I never did nothin' like that."

"It'll be easy to prove it," said Hackett. "The wife will identify the tie. With all five of the grandchildren's names on it."

"Names?" said Scofield stupidly. "Names? What you mean? It's just a pretty design. I like to dress up good when I take my girl out."

"Oh, for God's sake," said Hackett, "can't you read?"

Scofield shuffled his feet nervously. "No, man, I never could get that through my head."

Hackett and Schenke looked at each other. They practically never caught up with the muggers. And they could hope he'd tell them his pal's name. He'd just thought it was a pretty design and taken it as added loot to the few bucks in Hagen's pocket. That necktie was going to send him up for voluntary manslaughter.

Chapter 9

On Monday morning Higgins went to see the Ayers woman. She was a fairly good-looking woman with long blond hair. They were just getting ready to discharge her, and there was a friend there to take her home, a sensible-looking dark-haired girl. The Ayers woman couldn't talk, with her jaw wired shut, but she listened to Higgins' questions and scrawled in his notebook, *Don't want charge, my fault for not telling before.* The other girl followed him out to the hall. "This has been an awful shock to her," she said. "I've known Marcia for a long time—it used to be Mark, you know. She always wanted so bad to be a real girl, and have a husband to love her, and she saved up a long time for that operation. And now this is how it turns out. Is he going to stay in jail?"

"He'll be charged with simple assault and get something like thirty days," said Higgins.

"Well, I'll take Marcia home with me and patch her up."

The paperwork on the gang war yesterday was still going on. It was Palliser's day off. The lineup at the jail had been arranged for eleven o'clock, and Galeano went to cover it. The daughter brought Mrs. Ryerson in and she surveyed the lineup of men under the fluorescent lights and unhesitatingly identified Scott and Cooper.

She told Galeano that nothing had been missing from the house but some cash from her handbag. The daughter said, "Well, you're not going on living there alone any longer. You know we've got the guesthouse in back, you'll still be independent and a lot safer.''

At two-thirty a new homicide went down, and they all swore; they were still getting statements from those witnesses and would have to arrange a stakeout for the garage on Union Street, hoping to pick up Webb; all they needed was something new to work. Calhoun went out to see what it was. It was the body of a young man on the sidewalk along Leeward Avenue, and standing over it was Patrolman Dave Turner with a girl and another man. This was a narrow old street of small houses.

"What happened here?" asked Calhoun.

"It was Mr. Gomez called in," said Turner.

"You're damned right I did." He was a middle-aged dark man with a belligerent expression. "On my way to work, I work the swing shift at an assembly plant down on Florence, and just as I go to turn onto Hoover, I see this dame stabbing the guy right on the street in broad daylight, for God's sake. I jump out of the car and grab her, I look at the guy, and looks as if he's dead for God's sake, so I make the girl come with me and find a public phone half a block up and call in. I don't know what it's all about but I can swear I saw her stab him."

The girl just stood silent and shaking. There was a knife in the man's chest, a medium-sized plastic-handled knife.

"So let's sort it out," said Calhoun. "What's your name, miss?"

"Anita Serrano," she said. She was a pretty girl in the twenties, with long black hair. "He was trying to get me into his car, he was waiting for me, he knew which bus I take home, and I think he was high on some kind of dope. I didn't mean to kill him, I was just trying to get away from him."

"You knew him?"

She nodded; she was still shaking. "He's Pablo Nunez, he lives down the block from us—right along here. He's tried to grab me before, and I didn't want anything to do with him. I just carried the knife for protection, I have to go to work in the dark, I'm on the

154

night shift at a Denny's restaurant on Adams. I mean I was, I've just got changed to day shift. I was on my way home.''

"All right," said Calhoun, "is that his car?" It was an old Ford parked at the curb.

"I guess it belongs to his brother. They both take dope and I'm afraid of them.''

The car was registered to Esteban Nunez. Calhoun got Gomez's address and told him he could go on to work. "Well, I hope you put her in jail," said Gomez. "Stabbing a guy like that." He got into his car and drove off.

Calhoun took the girl back to headquarters. She told the story over in some detail and it sounded straight, but of course the only witness was Gomez, and he made it sound like a deliberate attack. She lived with her family up on Leeward, and said the Nunez brothers had bothered her before.

Calhoun had got Landers in on it, and when they got her version they talked it over, leaving her sitting beside Calhoun's desk.

"Who's telling the truth?" said Calhoun. "Gomez was a little way off in a car. And the autopsy will say whether Nunez was high on something.''

"Yes," said Landers. "There could be a short-cut."

"I had the same idea," said Calhoun. They went back to the girl. She had calmed down a little now. "Miss Serrano, would you be willing to take a lie-detector test?''

"Well, I guess so," she said. "That's that thing where it can tell if you're telling the truth?''

"That's right," said Landers. "In the hands of an expert. Have you had any alcohol today?''

"Oh, no, sir, the only thing I drink is maybe a glass of wine at dinner.''

"Well, it won't take long," said Calhoun. "We'll take you up now." They rode up to the lab in the elevator and asked if that could be set up. The accredited expert on the lie box was Palomar, and he left whatever he'd been doing to test the girl. She relaxed more under his friendly manner and went off with him to the little room with the polygraph machine. Calhoun had briefed him about

155

the case. They waited, and forty minutes later Palomar brought the girl back. "You can forget about the deliberate homicide," he said. "She was scared to death of being raped, she was just protecting herself the way she told you." The girl was smiling a little timidly.

"I never meant to actually kill him, I'm sorry even if he was no good. Will you arrest me for it?"

Calhoun said, "There'll be a charge of involuntary manslaughter, but it won't amount to much, Miss Serrano. I don't think you'll serve any time in jail for it. But I'm afraid we'll have to take you to jail, probably just overnight. You can call your family and tell them." Tomorrow she'd be released on her own recognizance, and sometime there'd be a simple hearing before a judge.

On Tuesday the paperwork was still going on, and the night watch had left them another heist. They wouldn't have seen Calhoun today anyway, his day off, but Hackett and Higgins had to appear at that hearing too, to testify to the circumstances of that shooting, and it was also Grace's day off; they were short-handed. There were now a number of traffic stakeouts at the garage on Union, in unmarked cars, hoping to pick up Charlie Webb. The A.P.B. hadn't turned up Albert Cruz so far. Galeano was in court covering Juan Diaz's indictment, and the bank heisters would be in court tomorrow, Scott and Cooper the next day.

When a new call went down at three-thirty, everybody swore, but business always got brisker during a heat wave. Mendoza went out on it with Palliser. It was a small single stucco house on Diana Street; the patrolman was Frawley and there were two women on the front porch with him, one about forty, the other older. They'd both been crying. Frawley stepped off the porch and came down to them. "The younger one's Mrs. Adele Ritter, it's her mother dead in there— Mrs. Esther Dudley. She came to take her shopping, she lives somewhere around here, she came in and found her mother dead. It looks as if she's been stabbed. The other one's Mrs. Minnock, she lives across the street."

Mendoza and Palliser went up to the porch. "I just don't know who could have done such a thing," the Ritter woman was saying distractedly. "To want to hurt Mother like that, to kill her, oh, I've got to call my husband—"

"We'll have a few questions for you, Mrs. Ritter. We don't like to bother you at a time like this, but you understand it's necessary," said Palliser.

"Yes, of course, I understand, but I've got to call Bob—"

The other woman was fat and white-haired, and they could guess would ordinarily have been a cheerful and genial old lady, but now she was pale and shaken. She said, "It's just nothing that could happen, Esther murdered. When Adele came to tell me I just couldn't take it in—oh, please, don't leave the front door open, officers, Timmy isn't allowed out."

"That's her cat," said Mrs. Ritter.

They went in and shut the screen door behind them. There wasn't an entrance hall, the door opened directly on a big narrow living room. The body was on the floor at one side of the couch, next to the coffee table, the body of a thin old woman wearing a blue nylon housecoat over her underclothes. "Good God, is her throat cut?" said Palliser. There was a deep wound in her throat and she had bled heavily.

"I think just stabbed with something broader than a knife," said Mendoza. "We'll see what the lab has to say."

There was a worn navy handbag open on the couch, a billfold half out of it. The cat was on the couch too, a handsome long-haired gray cat with yellow eyes. The room was orderly and neat except for the body, with comfortable old furniture, a black-and-white TV on a stand against the wall. At the farther end a door led into a hall, and at this end there was a door into the kitchen. Under the window opposite that door an artist's easel was lying on its side, with a small canvas beside it.

"Cómo," said Mendoza, and went to look at it. The canvas was about eight by ten, and the unfinished painting on it was a landscape with blue mountains in the distance. He squatted over it. "Some of the paint's not dry," he said. On the table beside the

easel were some artist's materials laid out, little plastic bottles of paint, a box with brushes of different sizes.

The kitchen was neat and orderly too, no dirty dishes around. The back door was open, and the screen door over it was unlatched. They went back to the front porch, and Mendoza told Turner to call up the lab.

"But she was perfectly all right at noon," Mrs. Minnock was saying. "I saw her come out to get the mail, and called over to her. We'd been neighbors for nearly forty years, I can't believe she's gone—like that. Some robber breaking in and killing her—"

"When did you get here, Mrs. Ritter?" asked Palliser.

"Well, about three, around there, I usually took her to market on Wednesday, but I've got an appointment with the dentist tomorrow, I said we'd go today. And I wish she'd have kept the doors locked, but in this weather, with just an electric fan—"

"Your mother was an artist?" asked Mendoza.

"Oh, just amateur, it was a hobby. I've got to call my husband."

"Our laboratory men will be going over the house, Mrs. Ritter."

"You can call Bob from my phone," said Mrs. Minnock. "But with police tramping all over the place—there's Timmy—"

"Oh, Mrs. Minnock, I can't take Timmy—" She was starting to cry again. "You know the children's allergies—"

"Now don't you fret, Adele, I'll take Timmy, he'll have a good home with me, you know I've always wanted another cat since I lost Maudie. Can I take him now?" she asked Mendoza. "He's never allowed out of the house, and he'll be terrified with strange men all over."

They let her come get the handsome gray cat, and she picked him up gently. "You come home with me, Timmy, you'll be fine with me. I'll take him right over and settle him down, I've still got all Maudie's toys and litter-box and all."

"Did you see anyone over here this afternoon?" asked Palliser. The woman hadn't been dead long. "Or could you say?"

"I was sitting on the front porch a couple of hours, my electric fan's broken. There wasn't a soul except Arnie."

"Who's that?" asked Palliser.

"Arnie White, he lives a couple of blocks down, it's a black family but they're respectable," said Mrs. Minnock with sublimely unaware bias. "Arnie does yard work for Esther, he did since he was just a kid and he'll be in high school now. He came to mow the lawn today, but that was just after noon." She went off with the cat and Palliser said, "That easel."

"Yes," said Mendoza, "we can read it halfway, John. He came in the back door and she heard him, and he stabbed her—with what?—just a sneak thief looking for what he could pick up? But with the doors open he'd have known there was somebody home. Anyway, it looks as if he knocked over that easel and canvas when he ran out. And the paint's still wet. It's possible he got his clothes marked up a little."

"The high-school kid," said Palliser. "I think we start there."

"Claro está," said Mendoza.

Marx and Scarne arrived in the mobile van, and Mendoza and Palliser left them to start work. The women were now on Mrs. Minnock's porch across the street, and they went over there.

"Did you see Arnie White leave?" asked Palliser.

"Well, no, I can't say I did. I saw him come about twelve-thirty, he used Esther's lawnmower, you know. He cut the front lawn first and then went round to the back, but my goodness, officer, Arnie'd never have hurt Esther, he's a good boy, it's a good family like I say."

"Where does he live?" asked Palliser.

"A couple of blocks down, it's a white house with green trim, I don't know the address."

"Bob's coming," said Mrs. Ritter. "He just thought the world of Mother. I still can't believe it's happened."

Mendoza and Palliser walked up the street looking for the other house, and midway in the second block spotted it. The woman who answered the door was very black, thin and tall, with gold-rimmed glasses. Mendoza showed her the badge and told her about Esther Dudley.

159

"Oh, my heavens," she said. "Why, that's just awful. All these criminals around—"

"We'd like to talk to your son," said Palliser. "We understand he was there this afternoon."

"Why, yes, he always did Mrs. Dudley's yard work, earn extra money. Arnie—"

He looked like his mother, tall and thin and very black, with a round face and kinky hair. He said, "You mean Mrs. Dudley's dead—somebody killed her? Gee, that's just terrible. It must have been after I left, I guess that'd be about two o'clock, there's not much lawn to cut, it didn't take me long. I never even saw her today, I just went and got the lawnmower out of the garage. She paid me by the month, see."

"You weren't in the house today?" asked Palliser.

He looked at them earnestly. "I never been inside her house at all, sir. I just did the yard work for her."

They were both thinking about that easel. He was wearing a pair of brown pants that had originally been a part of a suit, and a yellow T-shirt, and there were no obvious paint stains to be seen, but there could be minute traces which would show up in a lab examination. "Were you wearing these clothes when you were there?" asked Palliser.

He looked puzzled. "Yes, sir."

"Well, we'd like to borrow them for examination," said Mendoza, "if that's all right with you."

The woman was indignant. "You can't be thinking Arnie had anything to do with it, that's impossible, the robber came after he left there. Why do you want his clothes?"

Palliser said, "It could help to prove he's telling the truth, Mrs. White. Or it could if our technicians have a look at them."

"Well, if that's the case you can have them and welcome," she snapped. "Arnie, you go change your clothes and give the officers what you got on."

"Well, it seems sort of funny to me," he said, but he went away and came back in a few minutes wearing jeans and a different T-shirt and handed them the clothes.

"Thinking Arnie had anything to do with a thing like that!" she said.

They walked back down the street and found Scarne at the open door of the van. Mendoza explained about the clothes, the wet paint. "We noticed that," said Scarne. He put the clothes away in a plastic evidence bag. "I suppose those women were in and out of this house, I'm just going across to get their prints for comparison. The morgue wagon's on the way, she's been photographed and printed."

"You haven't come across a possible weapon?"

"Nothing," said Scarne. "Just from the look I doubt if it was an ordinary knife. Something broader and wider." He started across the street. Whatever they got on this would come from the lab.

Mendoza and Palliser went back to Parker Center. The day watch was just leaving, Farrell was shutting down the switchboard. He said, "Hackett called in about ten minutes ago. They hung around in court until nearly two before the hearing got called, and he said it was one of those fussy judges who wanted everything spelled out plain. They didn't get away until just a little while ago."

"Nice day off for Pat," said Palliser. "I hope to God something new doesn't go down overnight."

Nothing new came into the night watch until nine-thirty. Then they got a call from Communications, and what the dispatcher passed on made Conway swear volubly. He put the phone down and said tersely, "The werewolf."

"Oh, my God," said Schenke.

It was another shabby apartment house, on Miramar. It was after dark, and it was a dark street, but there was a bright moon and they could see how white and sick both the men were looking, waiting for them in front—the patrolman, Carlson, and the other man.

"He's Dionisio Morales," said Carlson laconically. "He found her and called in. The girl was Gloria Rodriguez. God, I'm glad I don't have to look at that again. This guy is really off his rocker. That room—" He swallowed.

Neither Schenke nor Conway particularly wanted to look at it either, but they had to, briefly, and it looked like all the rest of them. This time the head had been left on the floor, and the intestines were arranged around it in a kind of pattern. "Jesus," said Conway, and they went back downstairs.

While they waited for the lab van, they talked to Morales. He was a small thin man in the twenties, and his English was shaky.

"How'd you come to find her?" asked Schenke.

"I have the date with, *¿comprende?* Tonight, nine o'clock. I come see when I have money to pay, not often but sometime."

"When was the last time you saw her?" One thing the brief glance had told them was that it hadn't happened last night, the blood was too old.

He shrugged. "Three week, four week. I have job car-washing place Sixth Street, don't have much money pay girl. It very bad see girl that way—" He shivered. "All cut up in pieces. Bad."

"Was the apartment door open?" asked Conway.

"Sí, not locked. I have date, I go in—*¡Santa Maria!"*

"When did you make the date?"

"Saturday, the afternoon. I ring on phone. Not payday, but friend come pay me fifty he owe me. He owe for bet."

"What kind of bet?" asked Schenke idly, and Morales' expression went blank.

"Just bet, cards."

"Well, let us have your address." He gave that readily, Court Street. He had a motorcycle parked at the curb, and when they told him he could go, he rode off on it with a roar. They let Carlson go back on tour and stood waiting for the lab.

"And I could have a guess what the bet was on," said Schenke.

Conway said tiredly, "Cockfight or dogfight." Both were illegal, of course, but it still went on, even in the middle of town. There were places around with basements that could be fixed up for the fighting rings, and even presumably sane men retained enough bloodlust from the cave days to enjoy that kind of thing.

The van arrived and Duke got out of it with Cheney. They heard what it was and swore violently. "Why the hell can't you smart detectives catch up to this butcher? He's nuttier than a dozen fruit-cakes, you'd think anybody would spot him as the nut,'' said Duke.

"They don't always go around gibbering and drooling," said Conway. "We don't like it any better than you do, for God's sake. Take the pictures and print her and then you can call the morgue wagon so you won't have to look at it." Duke and Cheney started upstairs with all their heavy lab equipment, and Schenke and Conway started to ring doorbells on the ground floor. There wasn't a manager on the premises. Nobody on the ground floor, and there was somebody home in all six units, had known Gloria Rodriguez, or said they hadn't, and they seemed to be ordinary citizens, working-class people. Upstairs, there wasn't anybody at home in the two front apartments, but at the one just down from the girl's place the door was opened by a tall dark girl in a short terry robe. She looked at the badges and heard about Gloria and went green in the face.

"That one?" she said. "The one in the papers—cutting them all up? Oh, my God."

"Did you know her?" asked Conway.

"Yes. Yes, I did."

"Can we sit down?" asked Schenke. She led them into a small living room with cheap modern furniture, all in blond wood.

"I'm awfully sorry to hear about it," she said. "I didn't exactly approve of the way she lived, but that was her business, and I felt sorry for her." She sat down and lit a cigarette.

"She was a prostitute," said Schenke, and she nodded. "Can we have your name?"

"Mona Jarvis. Yes, she was. Personally, I'd rather die than earn a living that way, even when times are bad you can usually get an honest job doing something, but I guess the ones like Gloria are just lazy, figure it's easier picking up the johns. She told me she'd never finished high school, wasn't trained for anything, it was all she could do—well, that was just an excuse, ask me. My boyfriend, Jake, he didn't like me even to speak to her, but like I say I felt kind of sorry for her, she was pretty stupid, you know.''

163

"When did you see her last?" asked Conway.

"It was Friday night. I got home late, and I met her in the hall just starting out on the prowl. She owed me twenty bucks and the rent's coming due. I reminded her of it and she said she'd pay me back Saturday. But she didn't. I was a fool to lend it to her, that was a couple of weeks ago, but she said she'd been down on her luck and needed it for groceries. More fool me. And when I say that was the last time I saw her, well, I mean to speak to. When she didn't pay me I went up there on Saturday night but she wouldn't open the door. I knew she was there, I'd seen her come in with the john."

"Saturday night," said Conway. That could have been when it had happened, either that night or the next. "Can you describe the man?"

She said indifferently, "Heavens, no. I only happened to get a glance at them because I had the apartment door open, it was stuffy in here and Jake will smoke those damnable cigars. It was about nine-thirty, around there. I was just passing through the living room to get a glass of water in the kitchen, I just saw their backs, Gloria was unlocking her door. I couldn't say what he looked like, or even what size he was. He was carrying a briefcase." Both Schenke and Conway froze. "Why, what's the matter?" she asked.

"That was the Ripper, Miss Jarvis. Try to think back, doesn't anything come to you about him? Tall, short, blond, dark? Clothes?"

"Oh, my God," she said. "I just can't remember a thing about him—he was just the latest john she'd brought home. The briefcase—you mean—you mean he—"

"That's right," said Conway. "That's what he carries his tools in."

"My God," she said, looking sick all over again. "But I just can't tell you anything about him, I'm sorry."

"If you can't, you can't," said Schenke. "You didn't try to contact her again about the twenty?"

164

She shook her head. "It was Saturday night she was killed? No, I didn't. When I went up there, I made some silly threat, said I'd get Jake to beat her up—of course he wouldn't do such a thing and I wouldn't let him. When we were out together Sunday, I told him about it and he was mad. He said I was seven kinds of a fool to lend her money and I said I knew that already and I'd just have to forget it and write it off and let it be a lesson to me for the future. I'd just let it go."

"Do you have any idea where she picked up customers?" asked Schenke.

"Now that's a thing to ask me. Heavens, no. How do they? They used to be called streetwalkers, didn't they, but I can't picture Gloria walking the streets soliciting any stray male. I suppose she sat around bars somewhere looking for prospects, but I wouldn't know where. No, she didn't have a car." And there were a lot of bars on several main drags within a fifteen-block radius, and a lot more farther afield. "Do you know if she had any friends who were hookers too?" asked Schenke.

"She'd mentioned somebody named Isabel—once she said something like, 'I took a john away from Isabel last night'—but I don't know her last name."

And the casual rather stupid hooker, she probably hadn't kept an address book. "Well, thanks very much," said Conway, getting up.

She said soberly, "I certainly hope you catch up to that madman. She may have been immoral and stupid, and probably the rest of them were too, but nobody deserves to die like that, my God."

"That's so," said Schenke.

She closed the door after them. Down the hall the apartment door was open and they looked in to see how the lab men were doing. Mercifully the morgue wagon had come and gone, but there was still all the dried blood scattered around.

"Have you come across an address book?" asked Conway. Only one of the other hookers had had one, and they had wasted a lot of time talking to everybody she'd known and got no helpful results.

165

"No, but there are a few numbers on a pad by the phone," said Duke. He was on his knees dusting the footboard of the bed.

The phone was in the kitchen, a wall phone. On the tiny fold-down shelf underneath it was a memo pad with four names and numbers scrawled. *Isabel, Jean, Frank, Ruth.*

"Well, whether she took johns away from Isabel or not, they were evidently friends anyway," said Conway. "And that'll be for the day crew. I'm not going to wrestle with the telephone supervisor at this time of night."

On Wednesday, with Hackett off, they had that to work, and they all knew that it would be a lot of legwork for nothing, but it had to be done. This time there just might be something more to get on the werewolf. Mendoza got on the phone, was passed on to a supervisor, who punctiliously called him back to verify that he was bona fide police. "It may take a little while, sir."

"Just so we get the information eventually," said Mendoza.

She called him back half an hour later. Isabel's last name was Alvarez, and the address was on Bonnie Brae. The number listed for Frank belonged to the Black and White Bar on Temple, the number for Ruth was a beauty salon on Alvarado and Jean was Jean Dumas at an address on Eleventh Street.

They were about to split up and go out on that legwork when Farrell rang Mendoza and said, "A Traffic man just spotted Cruz's car a while ago, he called a backup and they've got the cuffs on him, they're bringing him in now."

"Oh, hell," said Palliser. "Somebody'll have to grill him, and we'd better contact those witnesses and arrange a lineup at the jail."

Galeano and Landers went to find Isabel and she was annoyed at being waked up, as she put it, at the crack of dawn. She started to cry when they told her about Gloria, but subsided before long and answered questions warily. She hadn't seen Gloria on Saturday night, but she'd seen her on Friday, they'd gone shopping together in the afternoon. "Where did she usually go, hunting the johns?" asked Landers.

"Anyplace. Around."

That was all they got from her.

Higgins and Palliser went out to that Black and White Bar and found it just opening. The bartender was a tough-looking man about forty by the name of Frank Sullivan, and he kept shaking his head and saying he didn't know nothing about Gloria. Higgins finally lost patience with him and said, "Come on, we're not Vice, we're investigating a homicide here, and the girl knew you, she had this phone number. What did you know about her?"

His mouth tightened, and after a minute he said in a quieter voice, "Okay. But I don't know a damned thing about the murder. I'm sorry as hell to hear about it, that bastard getting ahold of her. He must be a real nut, by what I heard. So okay, I used to steer some customers her way and she let me take it out in trade. That's all. She'd drop in here maybe three or four times a week, but she wasn't here Saturday night. That I can swear." And that was all they got from him.

Galeano and Landers had gone on to the beauty parlor. It was just a hole in the wall, a tiny shop on that main drag. Ruth was Ruth Herstein and she owned the place, had one employee. Gloria Rodriguez had been one of their regular customers. She came in every week, on Thursdays, to have her hair washed and set. "That's all," said Ruth Herstein rather regretfully. "No special rinses or dye jobs, she has this natural black hair, and she never went for manicures or face packs. But why are the police asking about her? She's got an appointment tomorrow at three o'clock."

"She won't be keeping it," said Galeano, and told her why. Neither of them had known she was a hooker, and were nearly as horrified to find that out as to hear about the murder.

Higgins and Palliser got to the address on Eleventh Street after lunch, so Jean Dumas was out of bed, if still in a frilly pink nylon housecoat. When they told her about Gloria she fainted dead away, and they had to give her a little first aid. When she was sitting up, sipping a glass of water, Higgins asked, "Did you see her on Saturday night?"

She was a vapidly pretty blonde with shallow blue eyes, a rather plump figure. She was too shaken to mind giving herself away. "Is that—when it happened? Oh, sweet Jesus, that lunatic—we all heard about him, but I said to Gloria, you could probably tell he's a lunatic, he'll have wild eyes or look like Frankenstein or something, you just got to be careful and size up the johns. But maybe he doesn't, is that it? Maybe he just looks like anybody else. Oh, my God, to think about Gloria—I heard he cuts their heads off. Did he cut her head off?"

"You'd just better not think about it," said Higgins.

"Oh, my God, then he did! Oh, my God."

"Did you see her on Saturday night?" asked Palliser patiently.

"Oh, my God, I did. Yes, I did. We were at Casey's Bar together for about an hour, I guess it was. I guess I got there about eight, I had dinner there and so did Gloria. We talked some."

"Did you see her pick up the john?" asked Palliser urgently.

She burst into noisy tears again, and between sobs she said, "Oh— Oh— Oh— I picked one up before she did— Oh— Oh— She was still sitting at the table when I went out with him— Oh, oh!"

Alberto Cruz was a very tough and experienced pro, and Calhoun and Mendoza didn't get anything out of him at all. It was two other fellows pulled that heist, he didn't know nothing about it. But the lineup at the jail had been set up for eleven o'clock tomorrow morning. Mendoza got on the phone to contact those witnesses to that heist while Calhoun ferried Cruz over to the jail.

On Thursday morning all five witnesses showed up to attend the lineup, and all of them readily identified Cruz in person; so Mendoza arrested him formally and went back to the office to apply for the warrant.

The Traffic watch commanders had been annoyed at Robbery-Homicide for taking patrolmen off the beat for that stakeout at the Black Colonels' headquarters, but at four o'clock on Thursday afternoon it paid off. Charlie Webb showed up at the garage, and two patrolmen nabbed him and got him in cuffs and whisked him away to jail before any of the other Colonels could start any trouble.

When he heard about it, Mendoza said, "No point in trying to talk to him, we'll have the evidence." Webb had been carrying a gun, a .32 Colt, and the slugs out of the bodies of the three Caballeros gang members were up in the lab. It had been quite a week so far, what with having to take time out to cover all the indictments. But they were always busier in summer, the heat fraying tempers to create the violence. The simple impulse to thievery went on all year round.

The Voice had become more and more insistent and compelling, and he was feeling confused and afraid. He had always obeyed the Voice. He wasn't sure, he never had been sure, who the Voice belonged to, some messenger of a higher power, some angel, or even God Himself. But now it was telling him, over and over, that he should reveal himself, tell about his discovery, the ecstasy of the blood. And he was afraid.

The one cold aware place in his mind knew that if he should reveal himself, other men would do terrible things to him because they were inferior beings who could not understand his enlightenment.

But just today, as he labored slowly over the calculator, the splendid solution had come to him. He could obey the Voice and still keep himself secret.

With the next one, he could delay bringing the blood, and prolong the surge of the ecstasy. With the next one, he would tell her all about it, all he had done, all the details of what he had done, and that would satisfy the Voice, but no one else should hear, should know. And afterward there would be the ecstasy of the blood.

Schenke and Conway sat playing gin on Higgins' desk while Piggott looked at real-estate ads in the *Times*, occasionally complaining about prices. They had just finished a hand at nine-forty when they had a call, and the dispatcher down in Communications was laughing.

"You've caught up to Jack the Stripper, boys. Go and get him."

It was an all-night gas station on Figueroa. The squad-car man was Costello and he was grinning broadly. "This time he bit off more than he could chew," he said to Schenke and Conway. "Oh, brother. Meet Mr. Swanson."

"That he did," said the other man standing by the squad. He was a big burly man and he wasn't young, probably in the fifties, but they could see the muscles standing out on his bare arms. "That he did. I haven't done any pro wrestling for ten years or so, but I still keep in shape. This brash kid walks in here, gets me to fill his tank, and then puts the gun on me. Like it's a big joke, laughing like crazy. I just slapped the gun out of his hand and knocked him out."

"How very nice," said Conway, "but where is he?"

Costello said, "Oh, Mr. Swanson was very efficient. He got him tied up tight before he called in."

Jack the Stripper, who had been plaguing them since the first of the year, was tied to a chair in the office with stout rope. "I always carry rope in the car for emergencies," said Swanson placidly. "Got in the habit when I was living in Michigan, haul people out of ditches in winter."

Jack the Stripper matched the description they had, about five-ten, dark blond. He was looking furious, and was calling Swanson every name in the book. It was nice to have this one cleared up. They untied him and put the cuffs on him and took him over to the jail.

On Friday morning as soon as Mendoza came in, Scarne called him and said, "This Dudley woman. Did she have a cat?"

"*¿Qué es esto?* Yes, why?"

"A gray cat?"

"That's right."

"Any other gray cats around the neighborhood?"

"I've got no idea, but this one was never let out of the house."

"Very nice," said Scarne. "Where's the cat now?"

"The neighbor across the street took him—Mrs. Minnock. What's all this about?"

"I'll tell you when I've done the rest of the lab work," said Scarne.

Mendoza raised his brows at the phone, said blankly, "¿*De veras?*" and went out with Hackett to take a look at Jack the Stripper.

Chapter 10

His name was Jeff Loftus and he'd evidently been reconciled over-night to his capture. He faced Mendoza and Hackett in one of the interrogation rooms at the jail. "So you finally got me," he said with a rather engaging grin, and shrugged. "Well, it was fun while it lasted." He wasn't bad-looking, in the late twenties. "I'm not a pro criminal, for God's sake, I suppose I'll have to serve a stretch in, well, that's how it goes and I've got no family to feel disgraced, I was raised in a Masonic orphanage. It was only supposed to be the one time, it was on a bet I had with Dick."

"A bet on what?" asked Mendoza.

He laughed. "I've got a good job, I'm a waiter at the dining room at the Ambassador Hotel, the tips are pretty good. Dick works there too, we live in the same apartment house. It was back in January, there'd been a story in the papers about this holdup at a market and Dick says it must take a hell of a lot of nerve to pull a thing like that and I said any fool could do it and he bet me I wouldn't have nerve enough, and I took him up on it. I thought of the clothes right off, you know—you feel sort of helpless without clothes, I'd noticed that when I was in the service and we came up for short-arm inspection." Both Mendoza and Hackett began to laugh. "And I thought about the all night gas station right away as an ideal place to hit. Well, I did the first one, Dick was hunched down in the back of the car to be sure I really pulled it off, and that

172

was supposed to be it. Only I got such a kick out of it," said Loftus, "I went on doing it. Which Dick didn't know." And there wouldn't be anything in an accessory charge anyway.

Hackett asked, "Where did you get the gun?" It was an old S. & W. .32.

"Pawnshop down on Third," said Loftus. "It's all legal, they made me wait while they checked with the police that I didn't have a record."

Mendoza laughed again. "Well, I trust you've had your fling at crime and won't be tempted to turn pro."

Loftus said reflectively, "I don't know, the take wasn't all that great, but it was the hell of a lot of fun."

Landers, Higgins, and Palliser had been wandering around all those bars trying to find out if anybody remembered Gloria Rodriguez picking up a john last Saturday night. It was nearly a week ago and so far they had drawn blank. They came back one after the other in late afternoon, and Higgins said, "We'll never pin it down. Number forty-three, my God. In those dives, who takes any notice which john the hooker picks up? Even if the Jarvis girl had noticed anything about him, it probably wouldn't be much."

A lab report came in; the slugs from two of the Latin gang members had been fired from the gun found on Charlie Webb. That warrant had already come through. The Serrano girl had been released on her own recognizance, and that hearing would come up when the D.A.'s office found time for it.

Mendoza perched a hip on the corner of Higgins' desk and said, "I tell you, he can't go on forever. There's got to be a break sooner or later."

"When he's got away with forty-three?" said Palliser.

"Because he's got up to forty-three," said Mendoza. He blew smoke at the ceiling. "There's a pattern to the mass killings. At the end those killers break, sometimes all of a sudden."

"Well, I hope to God you're right," said Landers. "And thank God tomorrow's my day off." He stood up and stretched. "I think

173

I'll take off early." There was only twenty minutes left of the shift. Mendoza went back to his office for his hat.

As Hackett passed Wanda's desk, Calhoun was just ahead of him; he paused and said, "Well, pick you up in an hour, beautiful, I've got reservations at a dinner theater."

"Fine," said Wanda.

Calhoun went out and Hackett regarded Wanda seriously. He said, "Listen, you'd better watch yourself."

"Don't be silly, Art," said Wanda. "It's just a date. I can take care of myself."

"And I'd have a bet," said Hackett, "that a lot of other girls have thought the same thing, with that one."

When Mendoza got home and greeted Mairí in the kitchen, he went down the hall looking for the rest of his household, and found Alison in her armchair over a lapful of three cats; baby Luisa was pursuing El Señor, grabbing at his tail, and the twins were sprawled over coloring books. They scrambled up and pounced at him yelling, and he said, "Quiet down, *niños.* I can't listen to both of you at once. *"¿Qué tal, querida?"* He bent to kiss Alison.

"I'll tell him," she said sternly to the twins. "I had a brainwave, Luis. Swimming lessons. They might as well learn to swim, and maybe it'll settle them down. I called the YWCA first, but they don't have any classes that include boys, but the local public pool in Burbank does. It's not very expensive, and there are trained instructors—"

"Going to learn to swim!" said Johnny. "It looked like fun."

Terry was bouncing excitedly. "We start Monday, we get three lessons every week—"

Mendoza said, "Well, that was an idea. That ought to satisfy them."

He was just in on Saturday morning when Scarne came into the office with a lab report. He said, "This was a funny one."

"On what?" asked Mendoza.

174

"That Dudley woman," said Scarne. "You thought whoever did it might have got marked up some way by the wet paint on that picture. Those clothes, the kid who'd been working in the yard, you asked us to go over the clothes."

"So what did you pick up, anything useful?"

Scarne laughed. "Something funny. We went over the clothes with the 'scope and the vacuum and there's no trace of paint anywhere but we picked up some hairs caught in the cuff of one pant leg. Cat hairs. Gray cat hairs."

"*¿De veras?*" said Mendoza.

"That's why I asked about the cat. And when you said the cat wasn't let out of the house, I thought I'd run a comparison test. All hairs have individual characteristics, you know. So I went over there to get some hairs from that cat, and got scratched up when I got them—it's a pretty cat—and they all match. The hairs in that cuff match the hairs from the cat."

"Oh, very nice indeed," said Mendoza. "And he said he'd never been inside the house." He brushed his moustache in satisfaction.

"Well, it certainly puts him on the spot."

"And thank you so much," said Mendoza. He followed Scarne out and caught Palliser just leaving on the legwork, and told him about it.

"Now that is a funny one," said Palliser, "but it nails Arnie. Let's go and see if we can get him to tell us about it."

At the house on Leeward Avenue, Arnie White was home alone. He let them in silently and Palliser said, "We've got a few more questions for you, Arnie. You were in Mrs. Dudley's house that day, weren't you?"

"No, I wasn't," said Arnie. "I never was."

"But we know you were," said Palliser. "There were hairs from her cat in the cuff of your pants, and the cat's never let out of the house. You see, our laboratory technicians can tell, no two hairs from different animals or people are the same. And those hairs were from Mrs. Dudley's cat Timmy. You were in the house to pick them up."

"Oh," said Arnie in a small voice. "Oh. You mean, it's scientific, they really can tell?"

"That's right," said Palliser. "That puts you right on the spot. What about it, Arnie?"

He sat hunched up on the couch for another long minute and then suddenly, incongruously, he started to cry. "Oh, Mom's going to be awful mad about it—and I'm just awful sorry, I never did a wrong thing in my life before—it was all on account of Stella—" He sobbed and got out a handkerchief and blew his nose.

"Stella," said Palliser.

"Stella Bailey, she's my girl. And she's never been to Disneyland and she wanted to go, neither had I, and I been saving all the money I earn for a long while so's we could go for a whole day and go on all the rides and eat at the nice restaurants and all. And then Mom had all the trouble with her teeth. She's divorced from my dad and anyway he hasn't got no money, and all Mom's got is what she makes doing housework for people. And the dentist cost an awful lot, and she said she was sorry, she'd have to borrow all my money, she'd pay it back, and I know she will, but I had it all set up with Stella, we were goin' to Disneyland next week, and then I didn't have no money to take her. I never stole anything in my life! And I'd never go to hurt anybody—but I—but I thought—when I was cutting Mrs. Dudley's lawn—I thought maybe she'd have some money in her purse. I heard her daughter say when I was there once, she shouldn't carry so much cash—so maybe it'd be a lot of money—enough for the day at Disneyland."

"You went in the back door?" asked Mendoza.

He nodded miserably. "I knew she always took a nap in the afternoon. I thought if she woke up and heard me, I'd say I wanted a glass of water. And I had the hedge shears in my hand, make it look like I was still working—and her purse was on the couch and I just picked it up when that cat jumped at me—it was on the couch and it gave a big yowl and jumped at me, and I guess I kicked it—and she woke up and come to see, she saw I had her purse and she grabbed me and called me a thief—and I was scared. I just wanted to get away, and I hit out at her—"

176

"With the hedge shears," said Mendoza.

He was crying again. "And then all the blood came—" He'd got her in the jugular by blind chance. "And I washed off the hedge shears with the hose." But the lab could probably find traces.

"Well, so now we know," said Palliser. "How old are you, Arnie?"

"Eighteen," he gulped.

"We'll have to take you to jail, you know. You can call your mother from there when she's home."

"She's out workin', she'll be home this afternoon. All right," he said thickly.

They took him over to the jail and booked him in, and went back to the office to apply for the warrant. "Damn shame in a way," said Palliser. "He's basically a good kid. It was more of an accident than anything else."

"If he hadn't had those hedge shears in his hand—" Mendoza laughed shortly. And the lab would probably find some traces of blood on those. "I'll talk to the D.A.'s office about it. I think they may decide to call it involuntary manslaughter."

They closed down the legwork on Gloria Rodriguez that day. It was hopeless to try to trace her back. When Jean Dumas had picked up her john on that Saturday night, Gloria had been sitting at a table in Casey's Bar, and the werewolf might have picked her up there or she might have gone on somewhere else to find him. They'd never know now. He was still just a ghost.

On one like this there was more work for the lab and for the doctors than usual. The lab report on it didn't come in until that day, and it didn't tell them anything new. Again, several latent prints had been picked up, but they weren't on file anywhere and they didn't match any of those picked up in the other dead hookers' places. There hadn't been any sperm stains on the bedding or anywhere else. Again, there was evidence that he had cleaned himself up in the bathroom, two bloodstained towels.

177

An hour later the autopsy report came in, and there was nothing new in that either. Evidence on the body that she had been bound and gagged before the torture, and any of the injuries could have caused the actual death, the disemboweling or the decapitation. The trademark, the cross carved between the breasts, had been inflicted before death.

There would be more indictments next week, Carpenter and Scofield. And the weekend nights usually turned up new business for Robbery-Homicide. They all trailed out tiredly at the end of that day.

Beatrice Tolliver left her apartment about nine that night. She was tired and worried and unhappy, and beginning to be frightened about the future. You drifted into things, she thought, as she plodded up the street toward Beverly Boulevard. You were young and pretty and life was fun, just one big ball, and you thought it was going to last forever but it didn't.

She'd got a job clerking in a store when she was seventeen, she'd dropped out of high school because it was a drag, and the job was a drag too, standing on your feet all day and making change. She'd been more or less on her own for a couple of years then. Her mother had divorced her father when she was ten, and by the time Beatrice got the job her mother was turning into a lush. The year after that she'd strayed into the path of a hit-run driver when she was drunk one night, and then Beatrice was on her own. And it was a lot easier way to earn a living, peddling it to the johns, than working eight hours a day in a store. It had been easier for a long time. She could pick up maybe two johns a night, at twenty-five each, and that figured out to more than she'd earn on the eight-hour job.

But that had been quite a while back. Now Beatrice was thirty-nine, and she'd always tended to pick up weight if she wasn't careful, she ought to lose about twenty pounds now, the figure wasn't so good anymore, and there were lines coming on her face that the careful makeup wouldn't cover. Just this last month she'd had too many of them look her over and turn her down. Damn it, she thought, all the pretty young kids all around, taking business away from her, but you couldn't blame the men, why should they pass up the pretty young ones for a woman nearly forty and looking her age, with breasts starting to sag and too much fat on the hips, and the amateur dye job on the hair?

But she'd only have about a hundred left after paying the rent, and the last three nights she hadn't picked up any business at all. She thought about the future and felt afraid. She'd just go on getting older and then she wouldn't be able to get any of the johns anymore and about the only jobs she could get would probably be doing housework or waiting on tables, and maybe she couldn't even get those jobs. God knew what would happen to her. Looking back, she thought angrily that she should have had more sense, back there when she was still young and pretty and life was ahead of her, she should have looked ahead and got herself trained for some regular job instead of drifting into hooking. Well, it was too late now. Whatever happened to her would be her own fault.

She went to the Black and White Bar first. The bartender knew her, knew all the girls came in looking for business, but he didn't care. She bought herself the cheapest thing she could, a glass of red wine, and sat over it, not drinking. After a while a man came in alone and sat reading a newspaper over a beer at a nearby table. She got up and went over there, putting on a big smile. "You like to buy me a drink, dear?" she asked, ingratiatingly.

He looked up and gave her a glance. "Get lost, sister," he said in a bored voice.

Beatrice sat down at her table again and drank some of the wine. If she didn't get any business tonight or tomorrow, she wouldn't even have a hundred left after the rent, she needed to buy groceries. She sat on for about half an hour but no more prospects showed, and finally she moved on to Casey's. She'd hardly got there and settled down over the glass of wine when he came in. He stood in the entrance of the bar for a minute looking around, the place was kind of dark like most bars. It was around ten o'clock then and there weren't any other hookers in, she knew them all by sight, probably they'd all already found some business.

The man came directly over to her table and said, "Could I buy you a drink?"

"Sure," she said, smiling at him. He was a different type than the usual ones she got, he looked as if he might be an office worker of some kind. He was carrying a briefcase. "Just another glass of wine," she said.

He got two glasses at the bar and sat down at the table but he didn't start to drink his. He wasn't bad-looking, clean shaven and not too old. He smiled at her and said, "What's the asking price?"

She said quickly, "Thirty-five." She could always come down.

"That's okay," he said. He had a kind of soft voice. He was all dressed up in a good suit, white shirt and tie. "My car's outside, we'll go back to your place. Finish your drink."

She was so relieved at the prospect of some money that she gulped the wine in a hurry, not noticing that he hadn't touched his. She followed him out and up to the car in a public lot. It was a pretty good car too, not very old, and she began to wish she'd said fifty. Maybe he would've gone for it. She got in the car beside him and told him where to go. "It's over on Second, just a few blocks."

He found a slot on the street a little way down and they walked back to the apartment. The building was quiet. The manageress spent most of her time watching TV and never noticed anything. Beatrice unlocked her door at the end of the hall and they went in. She noticed he was still carrying the briefcase, but she didn't think much about it.

When she came back from the bathroom, he was getting undressed, and he even took his wristwatch off. He meant to put it on the chest of drawers, but it fell onto the floor. He looked kind of flabby and white. Then he opened the briefcase and took out some rope and Beatrice thought drearily, oh, God, one of the kinky ones, but you had to put up with it. She let him tie her up. It wasn't until he forced the cloth gag into her mouth that she began to be afraid.

Then he showed her what else was in the briefcase.

180

And then he began to talk to her.

A market heist had gone down last night and the witnesses came in on Sunday morning to make statements. They all said they might recognize a picture, so Hackett took them downstairs to look at mug shots. When he got back to the office after settling them down with the picture books, he found Calhoun just on the way out, and Calhoun said tersely, "Number forty-four."

"Oh, Christ," said Hackett, and he didn't want to look at another one but there was nobody else in.

It was Second Street, another shabby old apartment, and the patrolman was Dubois. He said, "This time he left the door open. It's one of those efficiency apartments, just a single room, and when the woman across the hall started out to go to church, it was staring her right in the face. She came out screaming like a steam siren and I happened to be passing. She fainted on the sidewalk and the manageress took her into her own apartment."

"Call up the lab," said Hackett.

They gave it one brief glance and went to talk to the manageress. About all she could tell them was the woman's name, Beatrice Tolliver. If she'd known she was a hooker she wasn't admitting it. The other woman hadn't known her at all.

"Damn it," said Calhoun, "how long can this go on?"

"Twenty in Kansas City," Hackett reminded him.

"And sixteen in Boston."

The lab men came. "I don't suppose we'll get anything out of the other tenants but we do have to go through the motions," said Hackett.

That took up the next hour and of course they got nothing. They heard the morgue wagon come and go. As they came downstairs from talking to the last tenant, Marx came up the hall to them. He said, "The damndest thing. He left his wristwatch behind."

"What?" said Hackett.

"Well, here it is. A kind of unusual-looking watch. New brand to me. Anyway, you can see it's a man's watch, not very likely it

181

belonged to her, and it was on the floor beside the bureau.''

"I'll be damned," said Calhoun. "But what good could it do us?"

Mendoza looked at the watch on his desk and said interestedly, *"Como sí."* Isn't that pretty. What good can it do us? This isn't exactly an ordinary watch. It's an old one, not a nice modern quartz type.'' It was a rectangular gold watch with a gold flex band, and the maker's name was Gérard-Perrigoux. "Old French firm," said Mendoza, "and not many of them around. I think it might be just worthwhile, boys, to get a nice sharp photo of this and ask the *Times* to run it, asking anybody who might recognize it to call in. It's a noticeable watch.''

"I suppose it couldn't do any harm," said Hackett. "There weren't any prints on it, Marx said. I'll take it up to the lab.''

The witnesses to the market heist made two mug shots, so that gave them some more legwork to do.

By four o'clock Horder had produced several fairly sharp glossy prints of the watch. Nobody else was in but Higgins, so he took them over to the *Times* building. He saw the layout man and explained. "Public service," said the layout man. "And from what I've read you'd like to catch up to that one, all right. Well, I'll pass it on to the newsroom. We can probably get it in the morning edition.''

Just trying all bets, Higgins took another print over to the *Herald.* That was an evening paper with not as big a circulation.

The night watch left them another heist with two witnesses to come in, and it was Palliser's day off.

Mendoza was at his desk thinking about lunch when Farrell rang him, and he sounded excited. "I've got a jeweler on the line, a fellow named Dunning, he says he knows something about that watch.''

"Siga adelante, put him through!'' said Mendoza.

Dunning had a pleasant deep voice. "I just saw this picture in the *Times,''* he said. "Naturally, being in the business, it caught

182

my eye. I had that watch in for cleaning and repair about two months ago, Lieutenant.''

"The break at last," said Mendoza softly. "Or Nemesis. Where are you?''

Dunning had a jewelry shop and watch-repair service on the ground floor of a new high-rise building on Flower Street. Mendoza and Hackett got over there in a hurry. It was an elegant little shop with tasteful displays of jewelry in glass cases. Dunning was a spare middle-aged man with gray hair. He looked at the watch and said, "That's the one. I don't know why the police are trying to trace it''—the *Times* article, very brief under the picture, hadn't mentioned that—''but I'd know that watch anywhere. It was the first time I'd seen a Gérard-Perrigoux in ten years. I had it in—I looked it up for you after I called—on April twenty-first for cleaning and a new mainspring.''

"And who brought it in?" asked Mendoza.

"I've got that for you too. It was a Mr. L. G. Tuttle. I remember he said it was convenient that I'm in the same building where he works.''

"And did he happen to mention where he works?''

"Why, yes, he did. He went on to say that he's with this big insurance firm with offices upstairs, Acme Insurance.''

"*Basta ya, se acabo,*" said Mendoza gently. "Thank you very much, Mr. Dunning.''

The insurance company occupied most of the ninth floor. They rode up there in the elevator and at the reception desk Mendoza asked for Tuttle. The smartly dressed blond receptionist looked surprised. "Mr. Lionel Tuttle? If you want to discuss insurance I can get you one of the salesmen. Mr. Tuttle's in the bookkeeping department.''

"Mr. Tuttle, please," said Mendoza.

She gave them a doubtful glance and got on the inside phone. Suddenly Hackett said, "I'd feel happier if we had more manpower with us.''

"If he suddenly starts foaming at the mouth, you ought to be able to take care of him, Art.''

183

Presently a man came out to them from the rear offices. He was a medium-sized man in the thirties, with a mild-looking round face, light blue eyes behind plastic-framed glasses, sandy hair. He was neatly dressed in a gray suit, white shirt, and tie. And for all their long experience at the job, neither Mendoza nor Hackett was sure how to go about opening this gambit.

Hackett showed him the watch and said, "This belongs to you, doesn't it?"

Tuttle looked at the badge in Hackett's other hand, and just stood motionless. Then without warning he began to laugh, a high excited laugh. "I left it there, didn't I?" he said rapidly, and his voice went up another octave to sound shrill and feminine. "I left it there because the Voice made me leave it, and somehow you know it's mine—he made me forget because he wants me to tell— *The great whore that sitteth upon many waters— The evil woman, the flattery of the tongue of a strange woman*—but from the first, you know, I knew that if it was wrong God would have stopped me as He stopped Abraham from the sacrifice—and he wants me to tell, the Voice, he's been saying it over and over— I've got to tell I've got to tell I've got to tell—" He was shaking all over violently. They looked at him with unwilling fascination, a man falling apart before their eyes. "He wants me to tell—" The high thin voice was shrill. "Tell the world about it, about my infinitely superior understanding—" And then he began to scream, piercing and sharp, and the receptionist screamed too and ran away blindly, and people began to come out here. Hackett had him by both arms but he wasn't resisting, he just stood still and screamed.

Mendoza said to one of the men who'd appeared, "For God's sake, where's an outside phone? We want an ambulance here quick."

They followed the ambulance out to Emergency. When they got there Tuttle had stopped screaming and seemed to have fallen into a daze. They talked to two doctors about him. "We won't keep him," said the older one. "He'll go straight out to Norwalk to the psychiatrists. My God, I'd read about that in the papers. It's incredible but of course there have been others like him. We'd better sedate him for the ride out there. And you'd better tell somebody there to expect him.''

Mendoza and Hackett went back to headquarters and Mendoza talked to Dr. Shapiro at the Norwalk Mental Facility, gave him all the details. "We'll be waiting for him," said Shapiro. "Very interesting, I'd like to delve into his case history.''

And they would have to do some of that too, if just for curiosity's sake. Hackett got on the phone to that insurance company's head office, which was in New York. He got shunted around a little, and it was nearly the end of the day there, but eventually they'd get something from them.

Mendoza called Gearhart in Kansas City and told him about it, and then he got Prothero in Boston, just as he was leaving the office.

"Good God Almighty," said Prothero, as Gearhart had said. "A bookkeeper for an insurance company!"

"You wouldn't have looked at him twice, until he fell apart.''

"Thank God you got him. He's gone right over the brink?''

"As soon as we caught up to him, as I'd suspected he might. There's a pattern to the mass killers. You know, if he was working for the same company in Boston, or even if he wasn't, you might be able to trace him back, find out if there was any suspicion of mental instability.''

"I'll see what I can turn up," said Prothero.

When Higgins came in the back door of the house in Eagle Rock, he said to Mary, "We got him. The werewolf.''

"Oh, George, I'm so glad, you'd all been worried about that one. What a terrible thing that's been." Their own Margaret Emily came to be picked up, and she patted his face fondly. "Steve and Laura went to the library but they should be home any minute. I don't suppose any of those women were a great loss, but thank goodness you caught up to that monster. And how did you?''

* * *

185

Hackett got home to find the children chasing around the backyard with the huge mongrel Laddie. He went in and said to Angel, "We've got the werewolf."

"For goodness' sake, tell me how," said Angel interestedly. "What's he like, who was he?"

And Hackett said, "I think was is the operative word."

Landers and Phil talked about it halfway home to Azusa, and then Phil said, "To think we'll be out of that house and back to civilization by the middle of next month! I really think the apartment in West Hollywood might do, don't you? At least it's less than the house payments. The only thing I regret is leaving darling Mrs. Jacobsen, we'll have to find another reliable babysitter."

Galeano came in the back door of the house in Studio City and kissed Marta, who was taking a cake out of the oven. "We got the werewolf."

"Oh, Nick, that is good. Such a terrible man, it was like that one at home in Germany, the Düsseldorf Monster. How did you catch him?"

"Tell you in a minute." Stripping off his tie, he started down the hall.

"Don't wake the baby, darling."

"I'm just going to look at her," said Galeano peaceably.

Hackett called Palliser at home to tell him the news. Palliser said, "Thank God. That was a fluke, but at least we've got him." After he'd talked to Hackett for a while, he went to tell Roberta about it but before saying anything, regarded his family fondly, Davy on the floor playing with a toy truck, Roberta nursing the baby Alan.

They got some information from the insurance company on Wednesday. Tuttle had worked for them in Boston, where he'd originally been hired, for six years before being transferred to Kansas City nearly three years ago. Then last December he'd been transferred again to their Los Angeles office. He'd been first on the list for transferral because he was unmarried with no family ties. He had a very good record with them, had been a reliable employee.

They found the apartment in West Hollywood where Tuttle had been living, a curiously anonymous place. There was little in it besides clothes, the usual appurtenances, and a small collection of books. The battered copy of De Sade had been stolen from the Boston Public Library, and a couple of the others: There were all the books about the other mass killers, the bloodthirsty ones. Strangely, or perhaps not so strangely, there was no pornography represented at all.

When Mendoza talked to Shapiro at Norwalk that afternoon, Shapiro said, "Is he talking? We can't shut him up, and it's all very interesting but pretty damned horrifying too. He'll be committed to Atascadero as soon as the red tape's cleared away. If you're interested, all his fantasies have two clear threads running through, religion and sex."

"I'm not particularly interested," said Mendoza, "just so he's not out hunting more women to cut up."

On Friday, Frawley was on his regular tour when he called in a Code Seven to have lunch. At random he'd stopped at a new place, a coffee shop on Wilshire. He parked the squad and went in. And by God, there in a booth against the wall was that beautiful redhead eating a sandwich. The sketch was a good one, he knew her instantly. He went out again and got on the radio, called for a backup. Dubois showed up five minutes later and they went in to get her. There was a young fellow with her and they took him in too, delivered them both to Robbery-Homicide.

She wasn't repentant or even especially mad at getting picked up. She laughed at Mendoza and Higgins there in the big office, sitting with her knees crossed defiantly and smoking a cigarette. The boy was a tall gangling dark kid with a weakly handsome face. The big revolver had been in her handbag.

She told them without prodding that her name was Patricia Danner. The boy was Eric Talbot. She added offhandedly that they

187

both came from Manchester, New Hampshire. She was sixteen and he was seventeen.

"I guess Daddy's going to think twice again before he crosses me," she said. "Oh, I'll bet he's been wild! But I guess he's been punished enough, not knowing where I was, I expect you'd better call him. Ricky and I've had a lot of fun, but I just decided a while ago I don't want to marry him after all, he's kind of a bore to be with all the time, and he's scared of the gun."

"Well, gee, Pat," he said, "the holdups were okay but you didn't need to have shot those guys."

"And who is your father?" asked Mendoza. "Give me the number."

She started to laugh again. "He's Captain Bill Danner of the Manchester Police Department."

While they were on their way down to Juvenile Hall, Mendoza called back east and got hold of Danner. He sounded like a hard-headed sensible man. "Well, of course I've been out of my mind, and the Talbots too. Those two crazy kids wanting to get married, and when we wouldn't give permission, just taking off like that! They took a Greyhound bus out of town but we couldn't trace them farther. And you telling me about these holdups, and the shootings—my God, that's my service gun she's got! She's always been wild as a hawk, her mother died five years ago and I've tried my best but it hasn't been easy. What's going to happen?"

"They're both minors," said Mendoza. "There'll be a hearing, but when they've both got responsible families, they'll probably get probation and you can take them home. You can talk to her on the phone, and I'll let you know when the hearing gets set up."

"Thanks very much, I'd appreciate that."

Mendoza felt abstractly sorry for Danner, and didn't envy him the job of trying to straighten out that girl. If that was possible.

Prothero called him back on Saturday. "I've got a little more for you," he said. "I got Tuttle's Boston address from the insurance company. It's an old house in an old part of town, and some of the people who knew him still live there. He lived there with his mother until she died about seven years ago, and then alone. I even found a cousin of his, a nice fellow named Walsh. He said the mother was a religious fanatic, and Tuttle was always a queer one, a loner.''

"That figures," said Mendoza.

"Yes, but something else," said Prothero. "Tuttle sold the house when he was transferred to Kansas City. The people who bought it are still there, I talked to them when I was in the neighborhood. They told me that when they moved in they replanted the whole backyard, and they found hundreds of animal bones, apparently dogs and cats, buried all over. My God, Mendoza, did he start practicing on the animals before he graduated to the humans?''

"Por Dios," said Mendoza. ''Just be thankful he's tucked away where he can't do it again.''

This had been another grueling week with a good deal of legwork to do, and at the end of the shift he drove home thankfully. In the kitchen Mairí MacTaggart gave him a welcoming smile. "They had their fourth lesson today, and they're taking to it just fine.''

"Good," said Mendoza, and opened the cupboard and reached for the bottle of rye. El Señor came at a gallop, landed on the counter, and slid half its length, demanding his share. *"Gato borrachudo,"* said Mendoza. "You're a disgraceful drunk." He poured him half an ounce.

Down in the living room the other three cats were in a tangle on the couch, Alison in her armchair, Luisa playing with a stuffed dog, Cedric sprawled at Alison's feet. The twins had their coloring books out, but scrambled up to greet him.

"We can almost swim," said Johnny proudly.

"We can float and we're learning to kick," announced Terry.

"That's fine," said Mendoza, and sat down in his armchair.

Johnny nudged his sister. "Ask him now," he said in a hoarse whisper.

Terry came over and got up on Mendoza's lap and fixed him with an earnest gaze. At a rather young age Terry had found out

189

that few males could resist her melting brown eyes. "Daddy," she said solemnly, "when we learn to swim real good, *then* can we have our own swimming pool?"

Alison and Mendoza burst out laughing. *"Entendémonos,* now let's understand each other, *chica,"* said Mendoza. "I said no and I mean no."

Terry looked at him piteously and two large tears rolled down her cheeks. Alison was still chuckling. "That one's going to be a menace to anything in pants ten years from now. I wonder whether she'll manage to persuade you after all."

"Don't take any bets on it," said Mendoza.